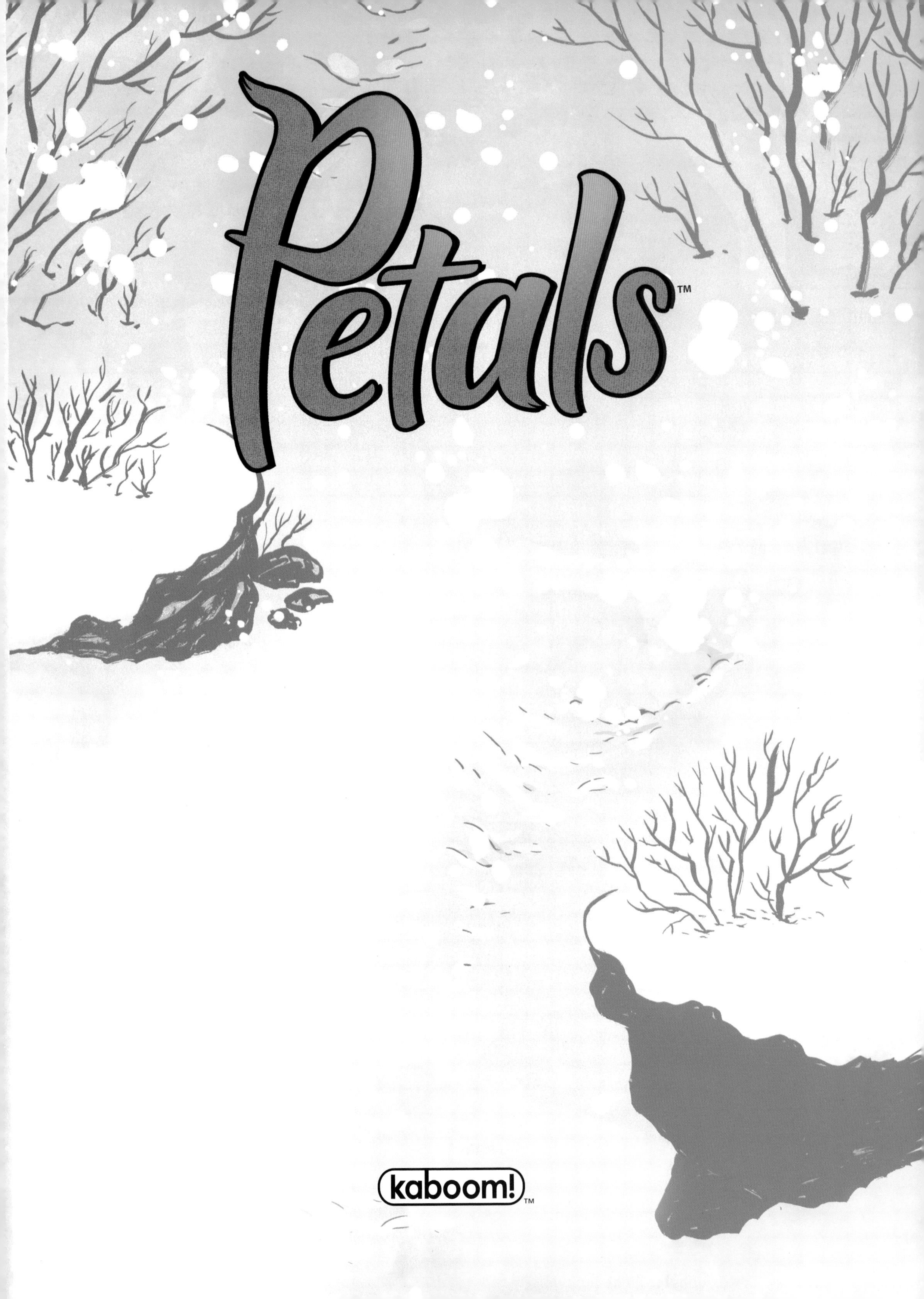
Petals™
kaboom!™

ROSS RICHIE CEO & FOUNDER
MATT GAGNON EDITOR-IN-CHIEF
FILIP SABLIK PRESIDENT OF PUBLISHING & MARKETING
STEPHEN CHRISTY PRESIDENT OF DEVELOPMENT
LANCE KREITER VP OF LICENSING & MERCHANDISING
PHIL BARBARO VP OF FINANCE
ARUNE SINGH VP OF MARKETING
BRYCE CARLSON MANAGING EDITOR
SCOTT NEWMAN PRODUCTION DESIGN MANAGER
KATE HENNING OPERATIONS MANAGER
SPENCER SIMPSON SALES MANAGER
SIERRA HAHN SENIOR EDITOR
DAFNA PLEBAN EDITOR, TALENT DEVELOPMENT
SHANNON WATTERS EDITOR
ERIC HARBURN EDITOR
WHITNEY LEOPARD EDITOR
CAMERON CHITTOCK EDITOR
CHRIS ROSA ASSOCIATE EDITOR
MATTHEW LEVINE ASSOCIATE EDITOR
SOPHIE PHILIPS-ROBERTS ASSISTANT EDITOR
GAVIN GRONENTHAL ASSISTANT EDITOR
MICHAEL MOCCIO ASSISTANT EDITOR
AMANDA LAFRANCO EXECUTIVE ASSISTANT
KATALINA HOLLAND EDITORIAL ADMINISTRATIVE ASSISTANT
JILLIAN CRAB DESIGN COORDINATOR
MICHELLE ANKLEY DESIGN COORDINATOR
KARA LEOPARD PRODUCTION DESIGNER
MARIE KRUPINA PRODUCTION DESIGNER
GRACE PARK PRODUCTION DESIGN ASSISTANT
CHELSEA ROBERTS PRODUCTION DESIGN ASSISTANT
ELIZABETH LOUGHRIDGE ACCOUNTING COORDINATOR
STEPHANIE HOCUTT SOCIAL MEDIA COORDINATOR
JOSÉ MEZA EVENT COORDINATOR
HOLLY AITCHISON OPERATIONS COORDINATOR
MEGAN CHRISTOPHER OPERATIONS ASSISTANT
RODRIGO HERNANDEZ MAILROOM ASSISTANT
MORGAN PERRY DIRECT MARKET REPRESENTATIVE
CAT O'GRADY MARKETING ASSISTANT
CORNELIA TZANA PUBLICITY ASSISTANT
LIZ ALMENDAREZ ACCOUNTING ADMINISTRATIVE ASSISTANT

PETALS, SEPTEMBER 2018. PUBLISHED BY KABOOM!, A DIVISION OF BOOM ENTERTAINMENT, INC. PETALS IS ™ & © 2018 GUSTAVO BORGES AND MARSUPIAL EDITORA. ALL RIGHTS RESERVED. KABOOM!™ AND THE KABOOM! LOGO ARE TRADEMARKS OF BOOM ENTERTAINMENT, INC., REGISTERED IN VARIOUS COUNTRIES AND CATEGORIES. ALL CHARACTERS, EVENTS, AND INSTITUTIONS DEPICTED HEREIN ARE FICTIONAL. ANY SIMILARITY BETWEEN ANY OF THE NAMES, CHARACTERS, PERSONS, EVENTS, AND/OR INSTITUTIONS IN THIS PUBLICATION TO ACTUAL NAMES, CHARACTERS, AND PERSONS, WHETHER LIVING OR DEAD, EVENTS, AND/OR INSTITUTIONS IS UNINTENDED AND PURELY COINCIDENTAL. KABOOM! DOES NOT READ OR ACCEPT UNSOLICITED SUBMISSIONS OF IDEAS, STORIES, OR ARTWORK.

ORIGINALLY PUBLISHED IN BRAZIL BY MARSUPIAL EDITORA IN 2017.

BOOM! STUDIOS, 5670 WILSHIRE BOULEVARD, SUITE 400, LOS ANGELES, CA 90036-5679. PRINTED IN CHINA. FIRST PRINTING.

ISBN: 978-1-68415-234-6, EISBN: 978-1-64144-096-7

COVER BY GUSTAVO BORGES

DESIGNERS KARA LEOPARD & JILLIAN CRAB

EDITOR WHITNEY LEOPARD

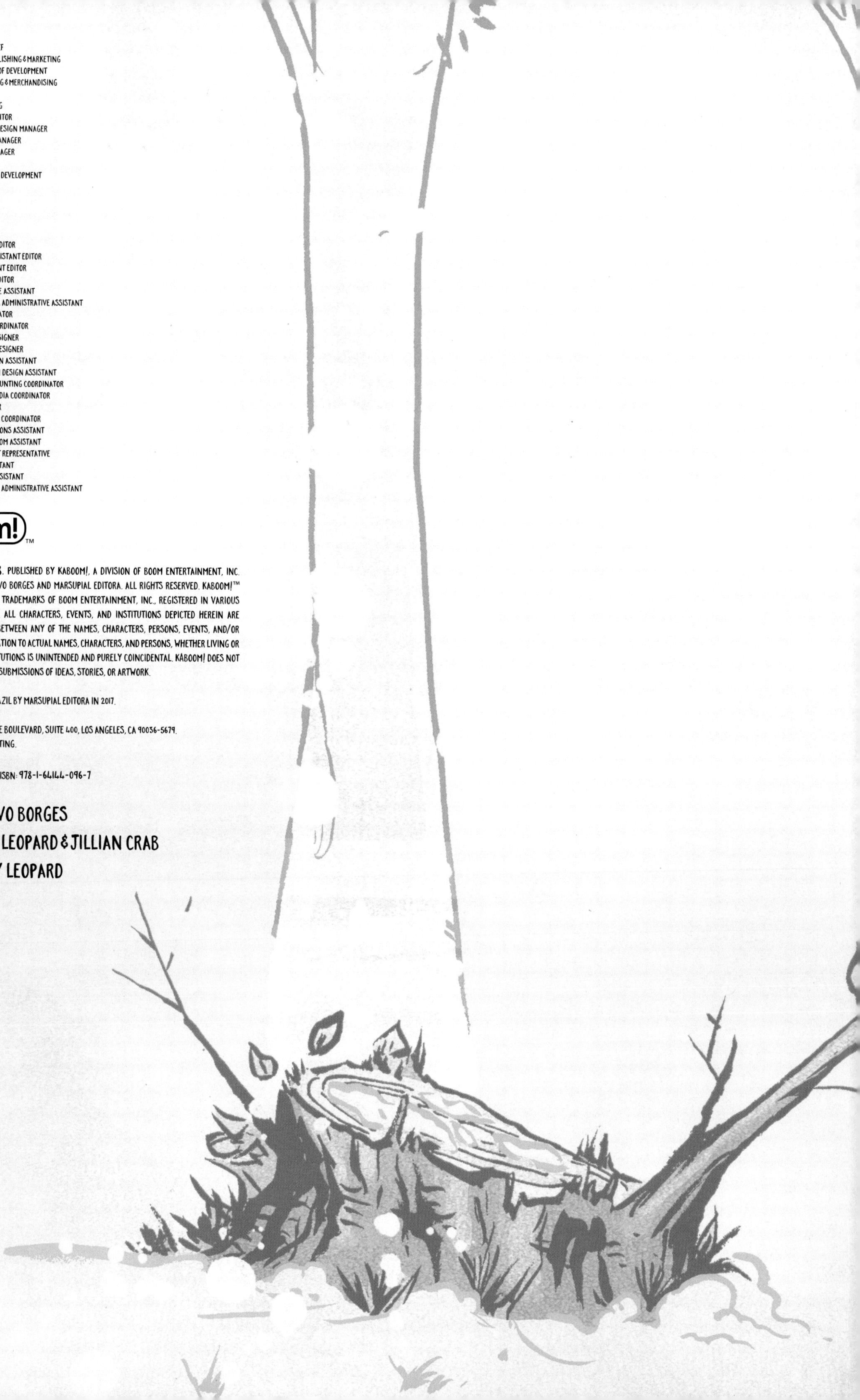

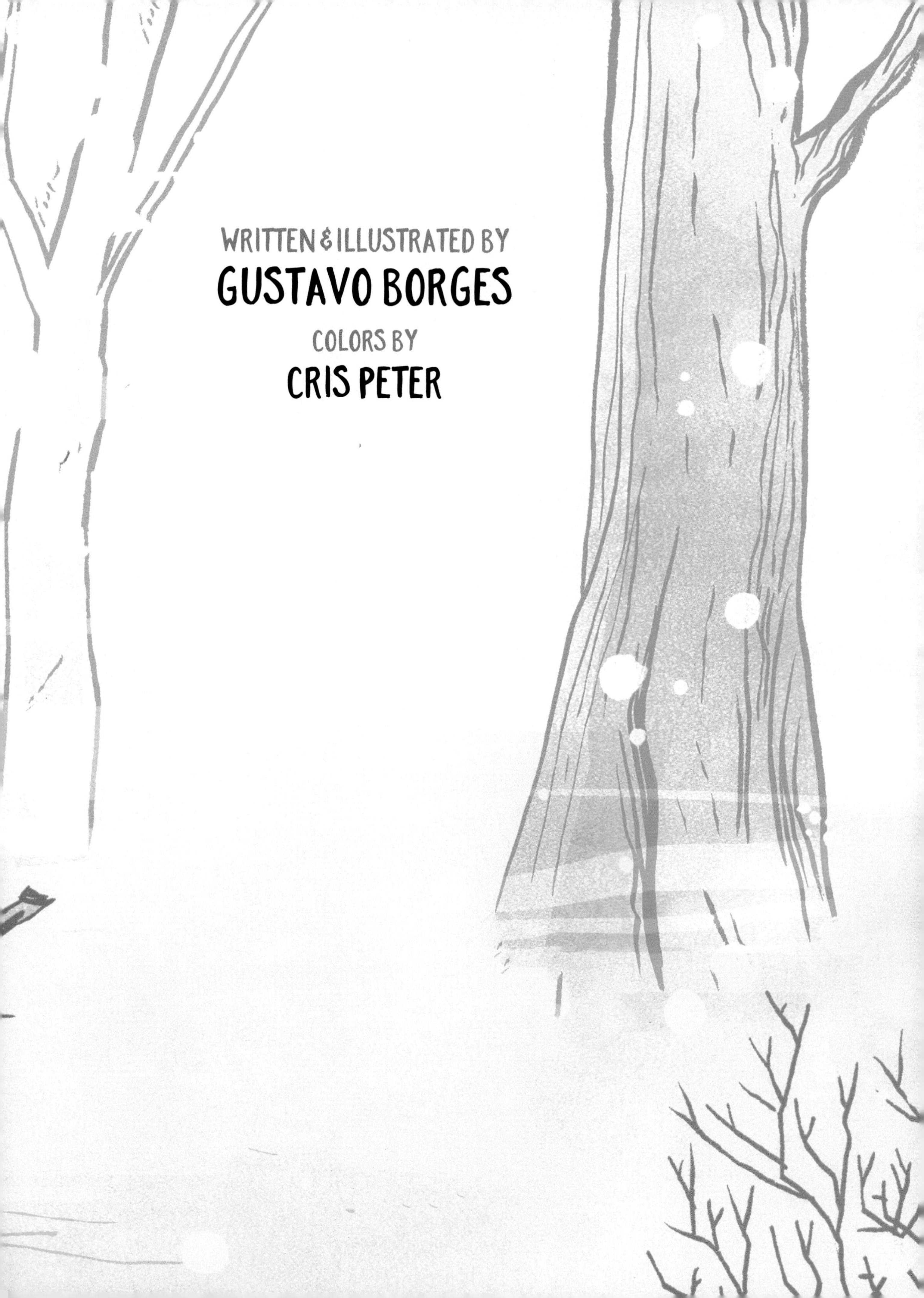

WRITTEN & ILLUSTRATED BY
GUSTAVO BORGES
COLORS BY
CRIS PETER

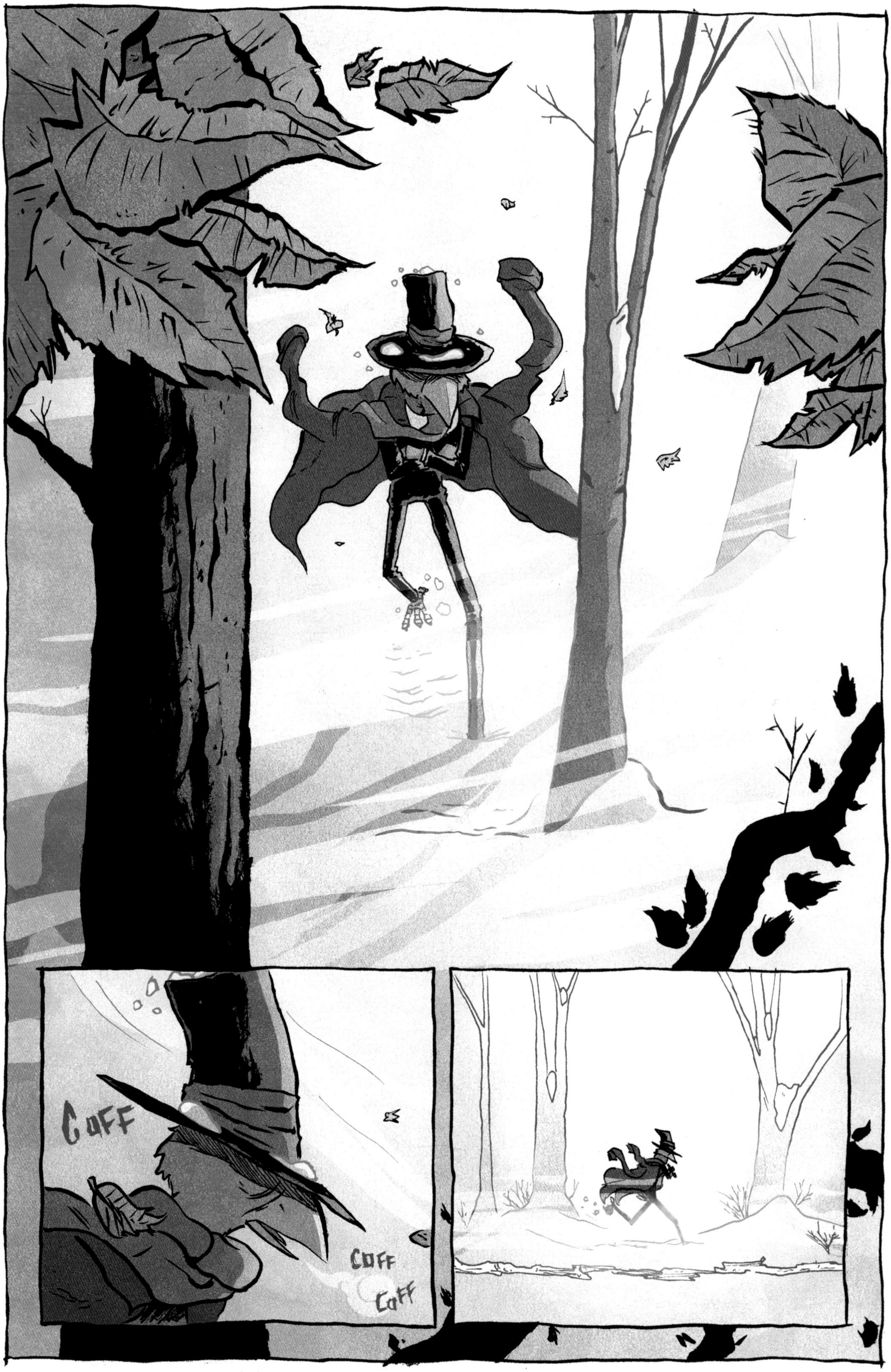
COFF
COFF
COFF

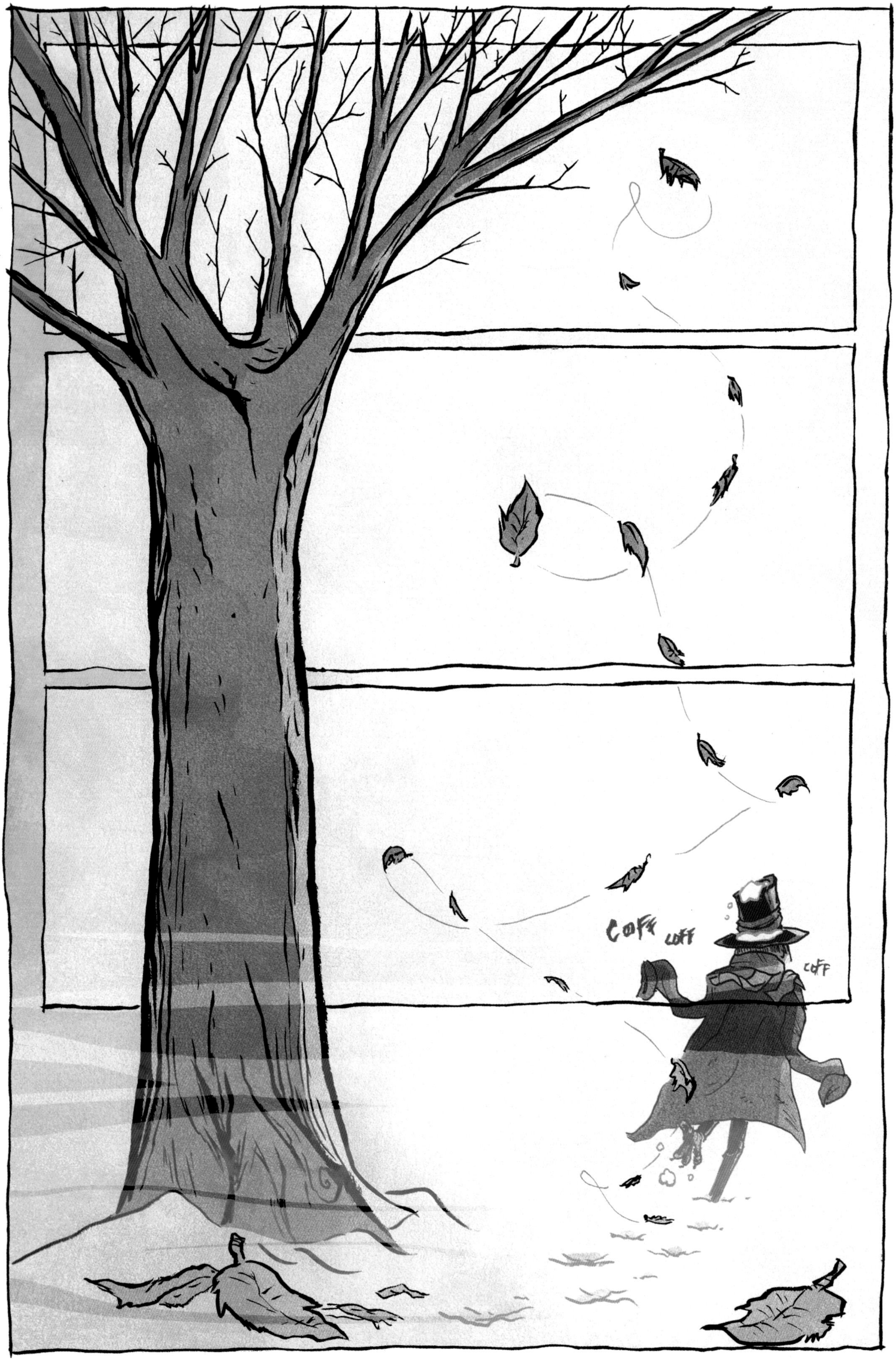
COFF
COFF
COFF

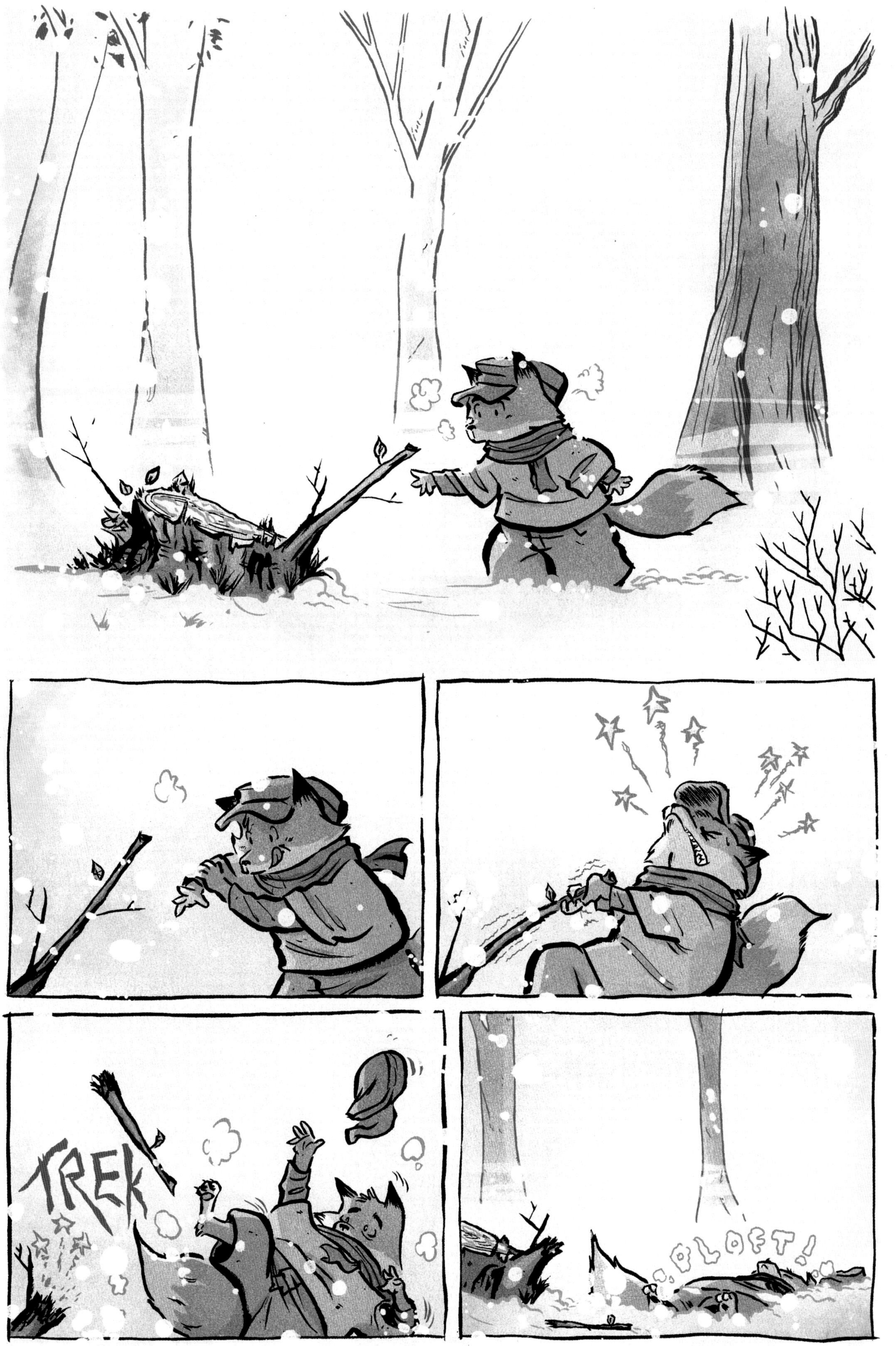
TREK
PLOFT!

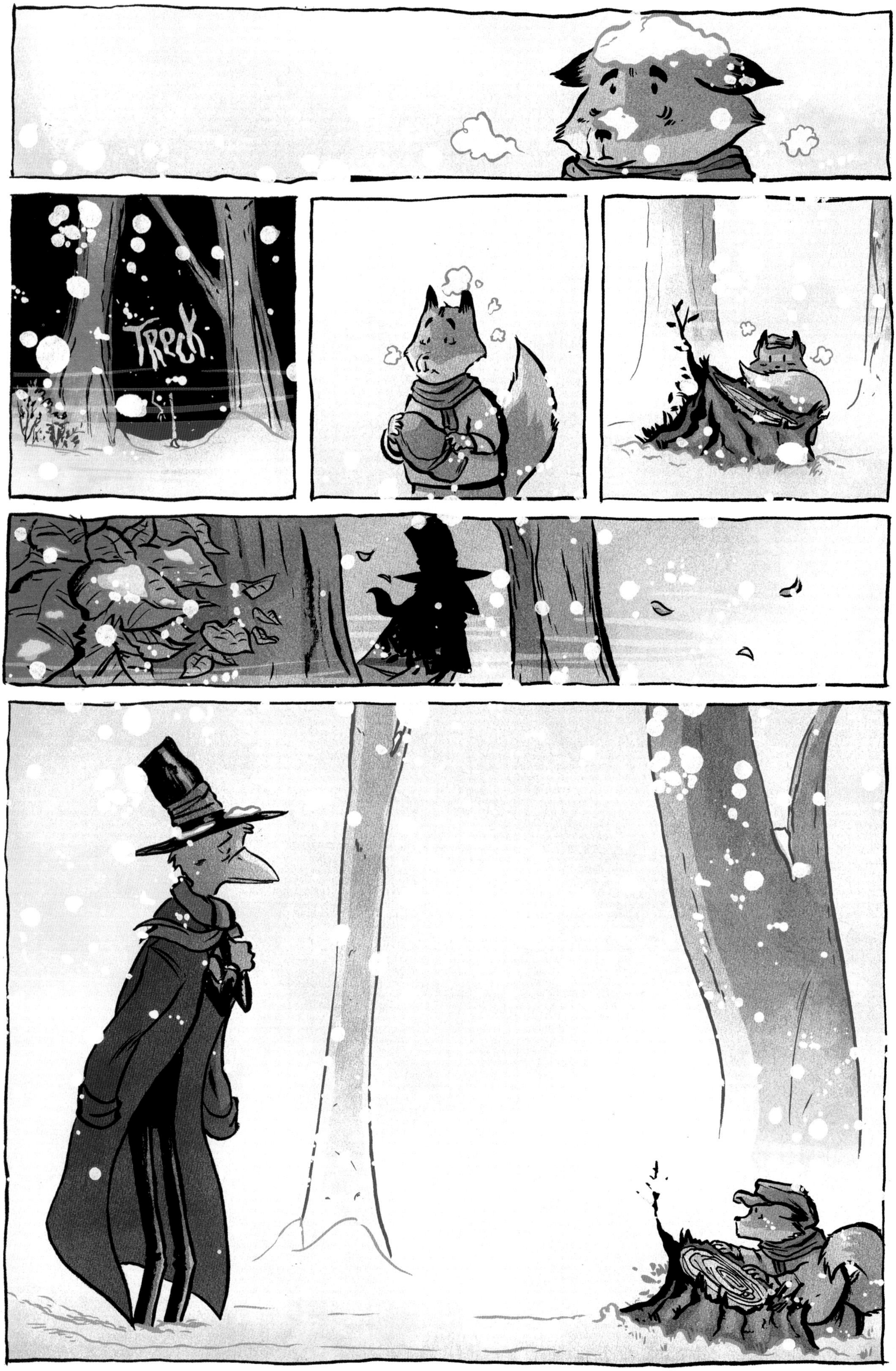
TRECK

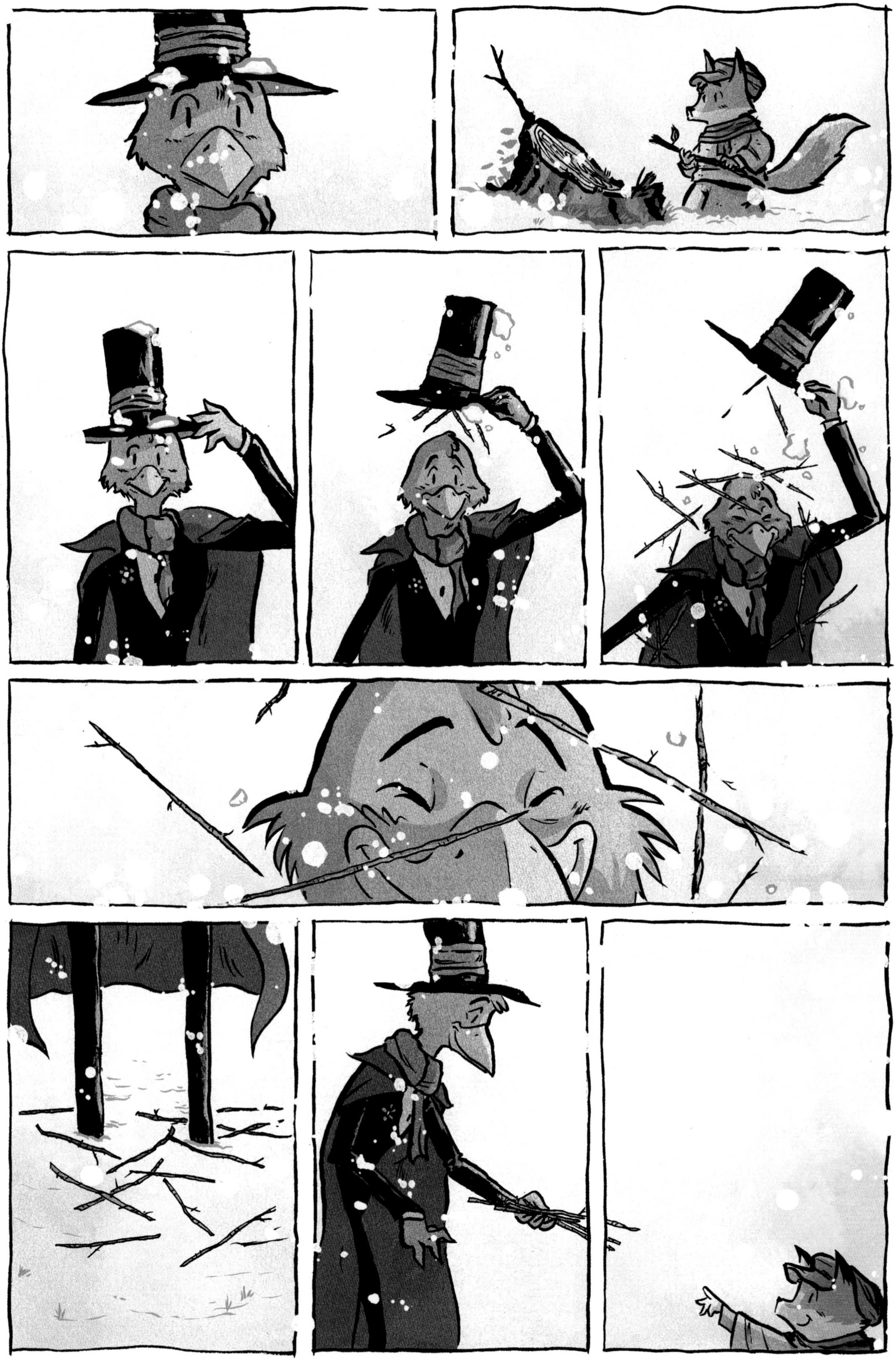

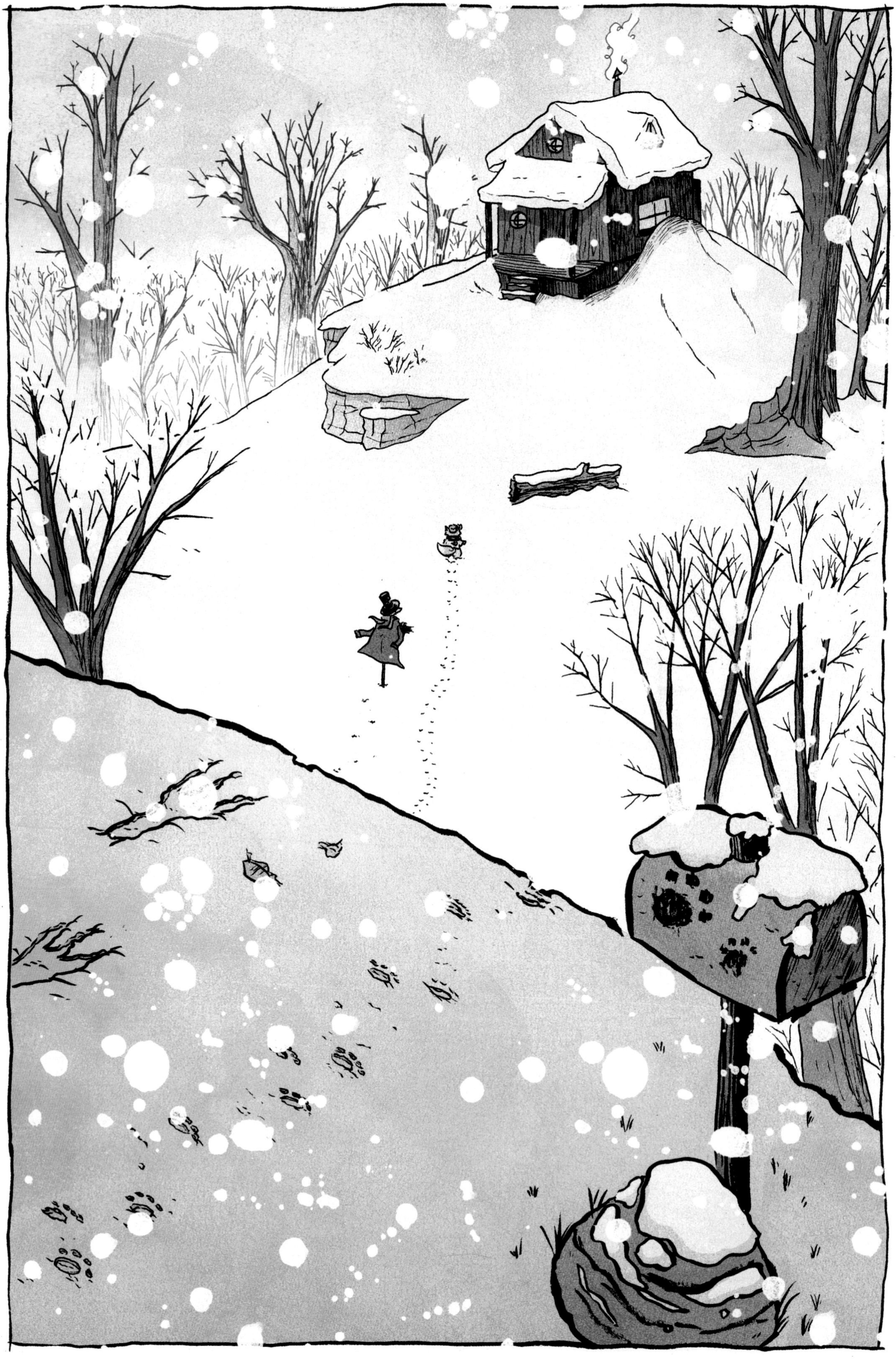

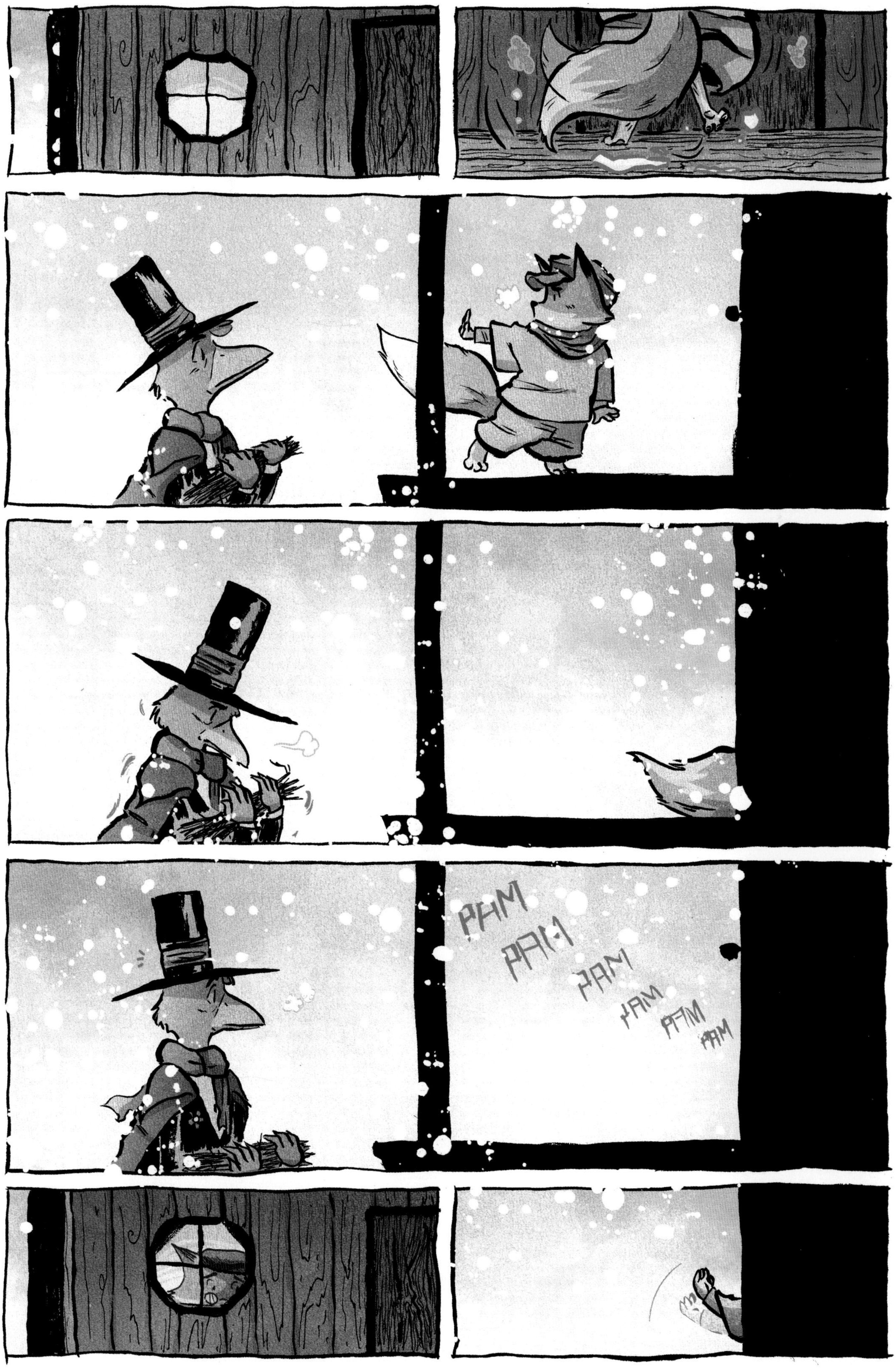
PAM
PAM
PAM
PAM
PAM
PAM

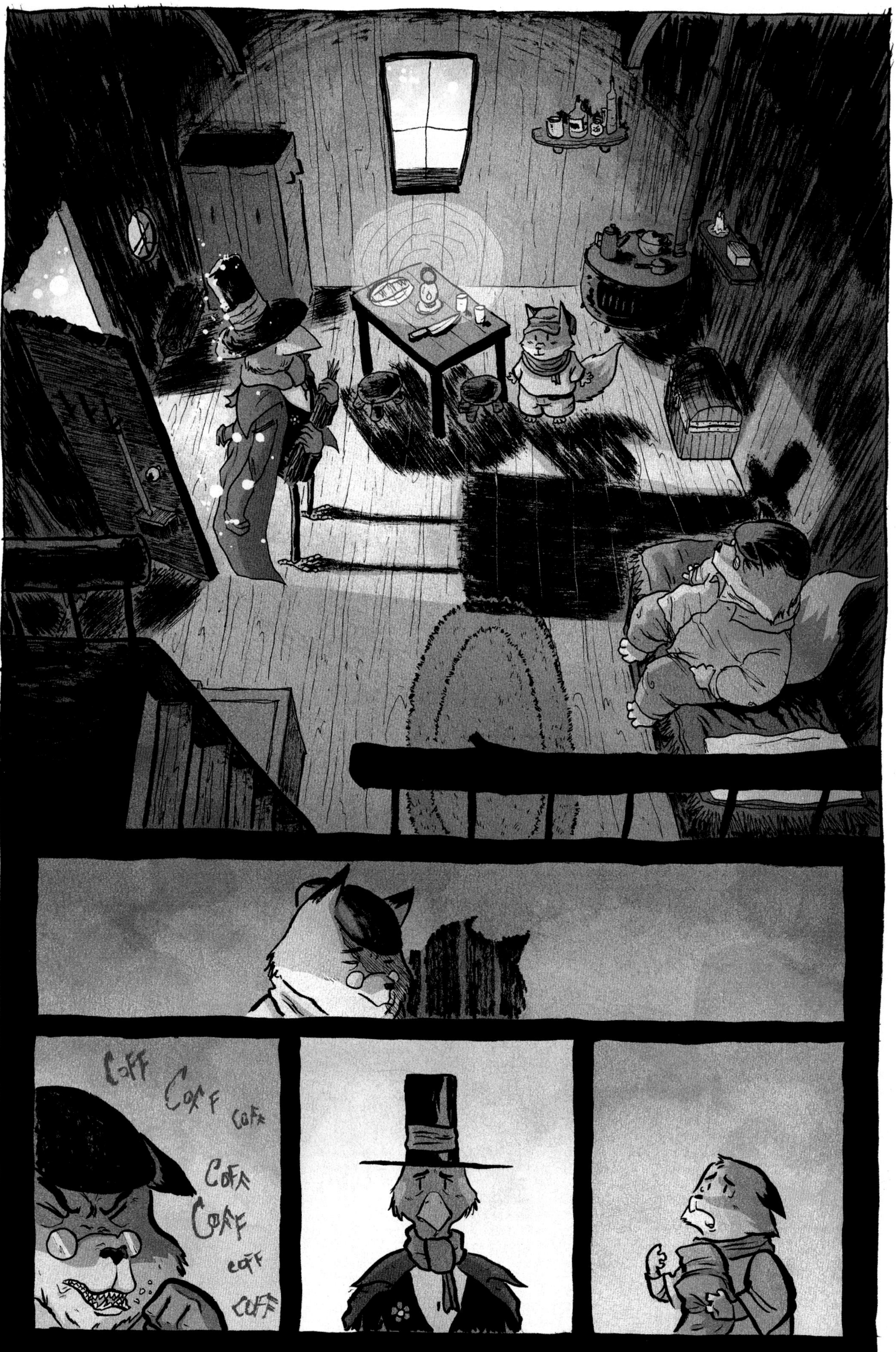
COFF
COFF
COFF
COFF
COFF
cOFF
COFF

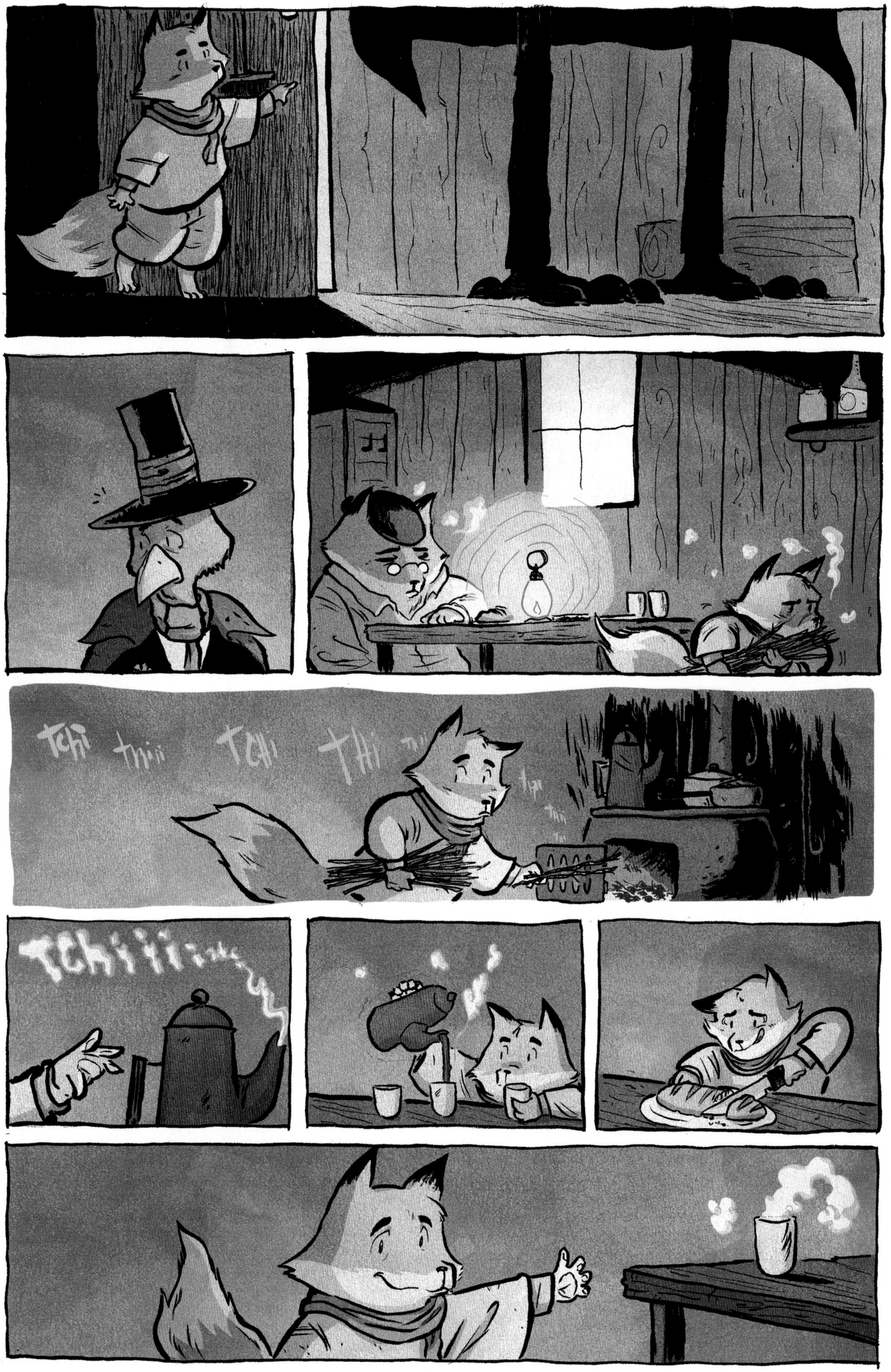

Tchi
thiii
TCHi
THi
Tchiiii

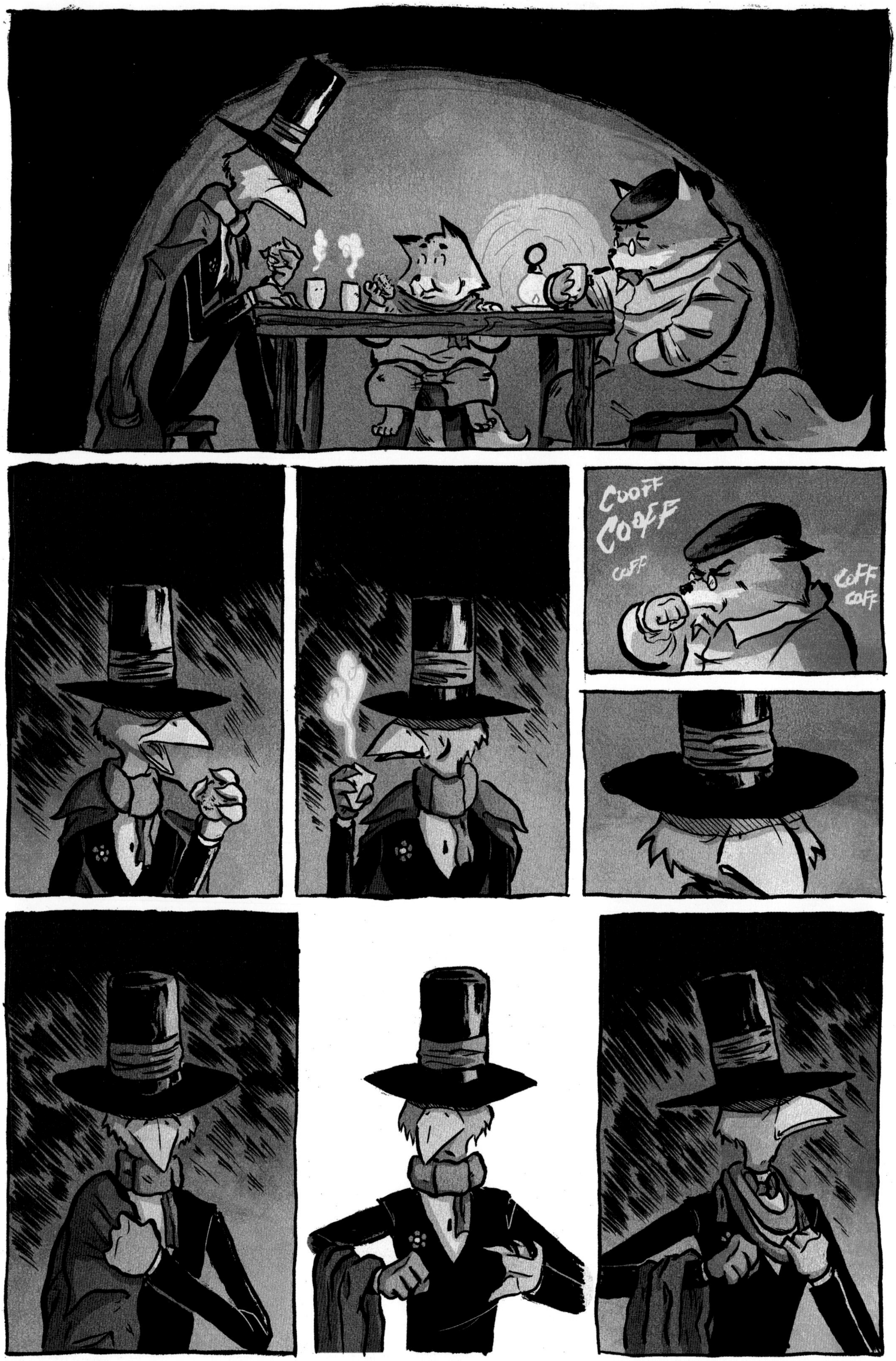
COOFF
COFF
COFF
COFF
COFF

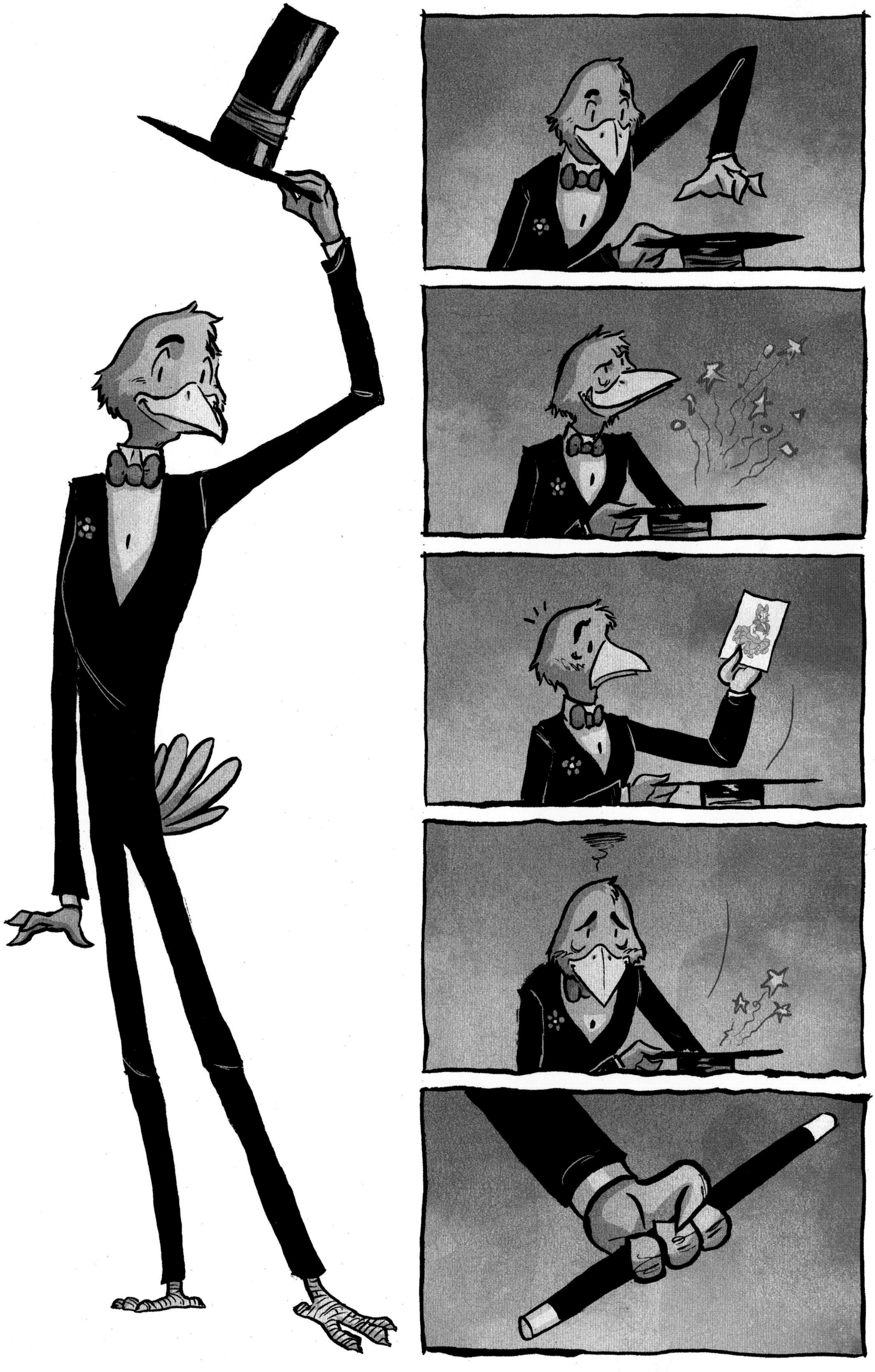

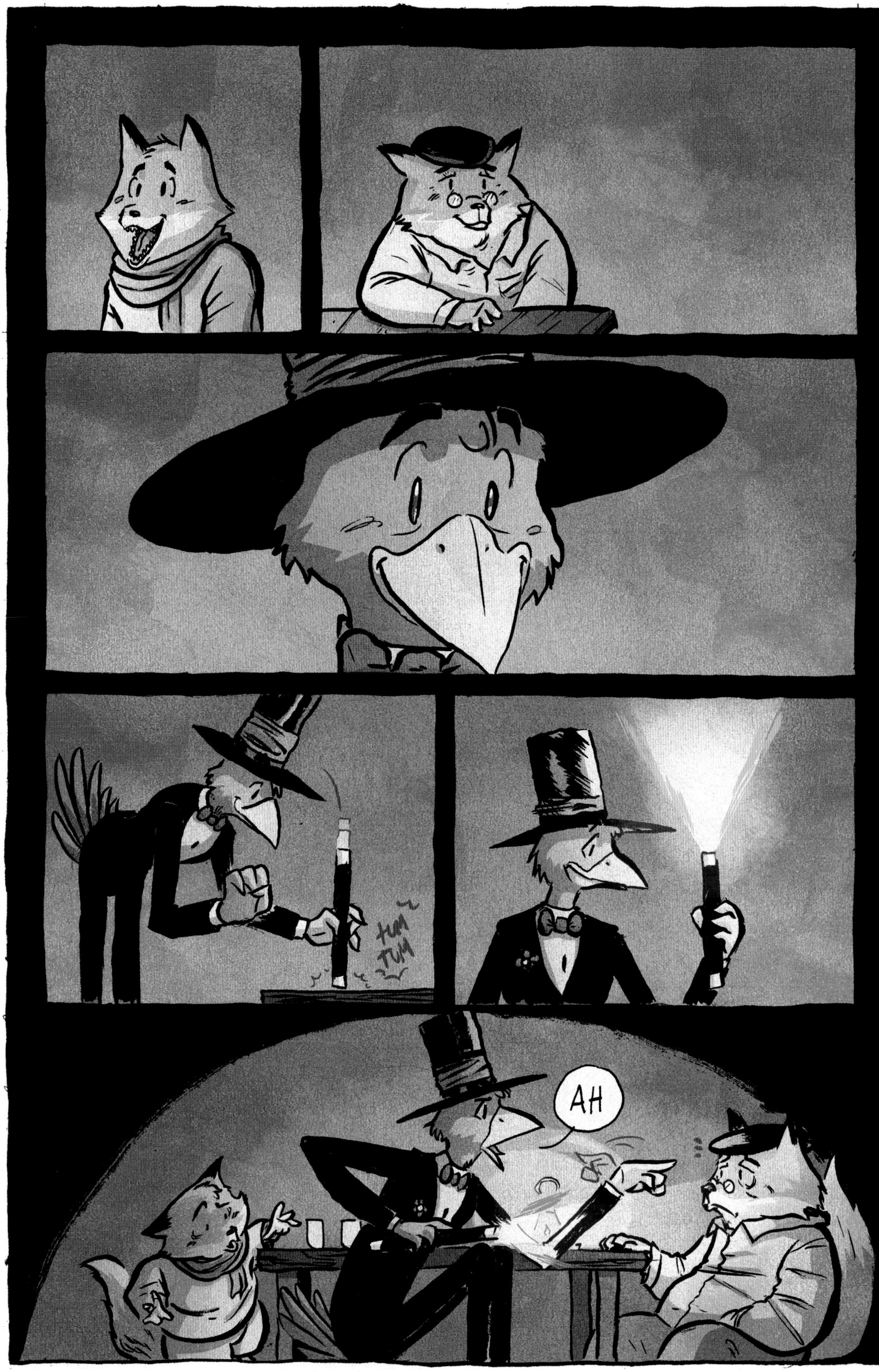
TUM
TUM
AH

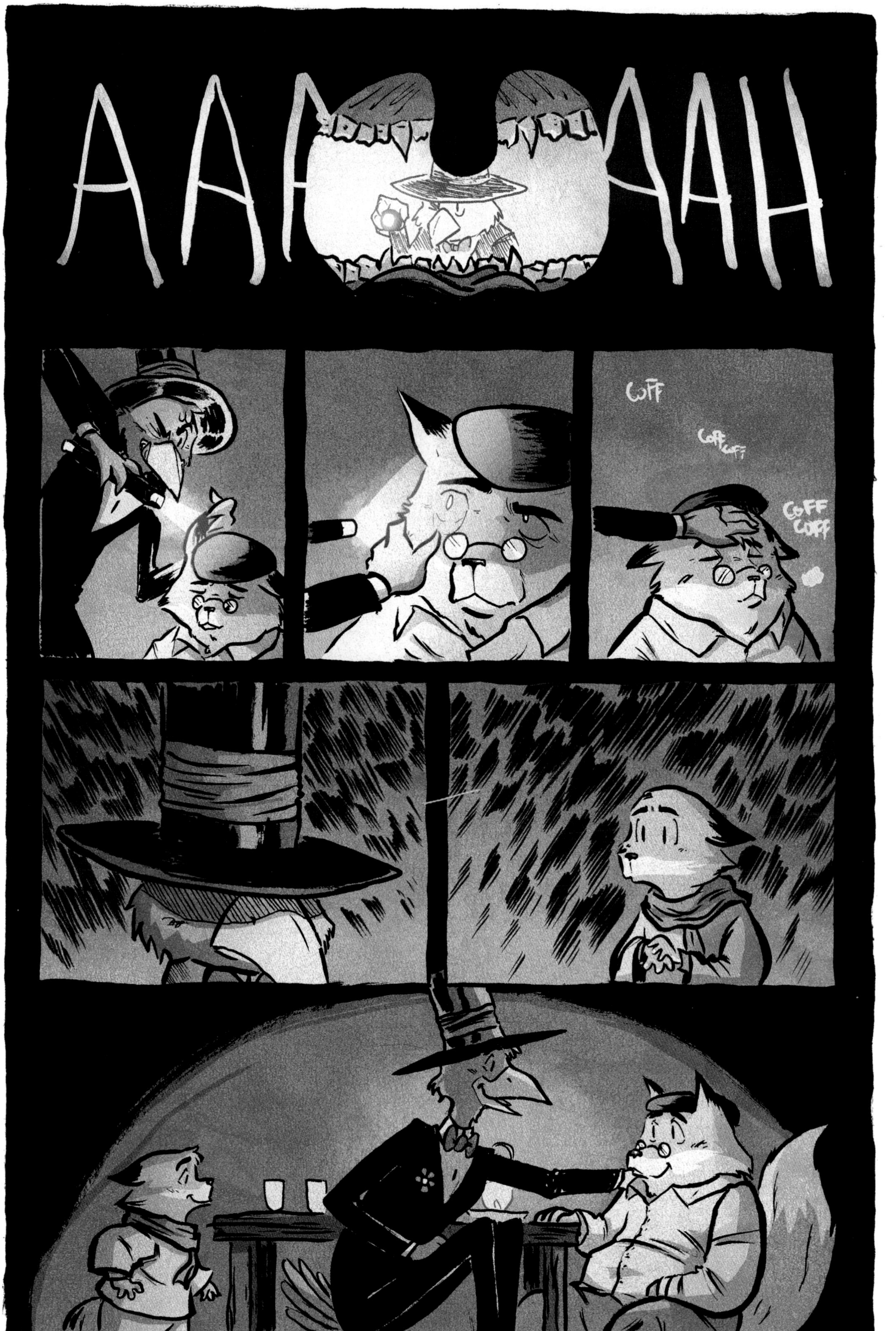
AAAAAAH
COFF
COFF COFF
COFF
COFF

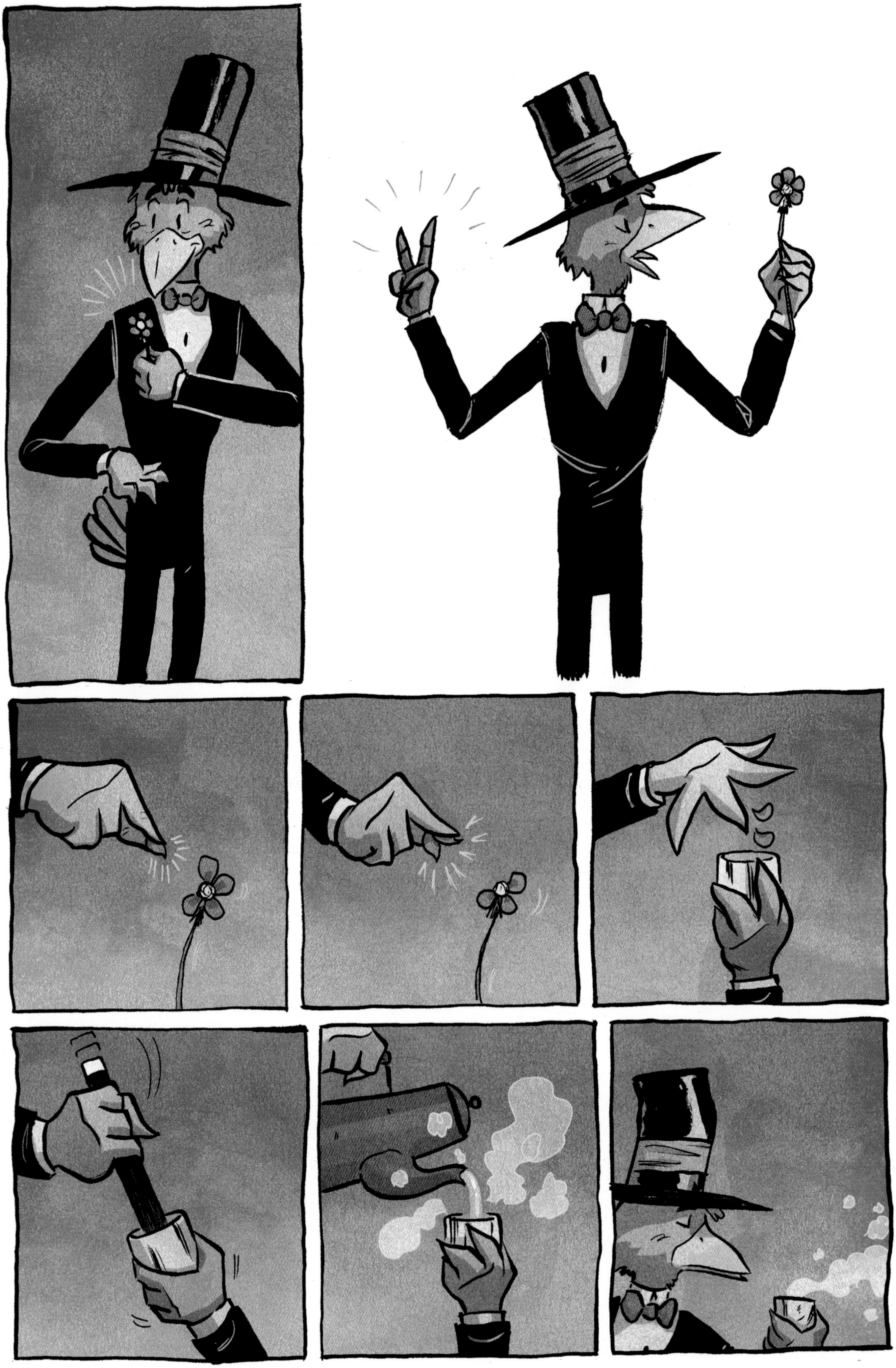

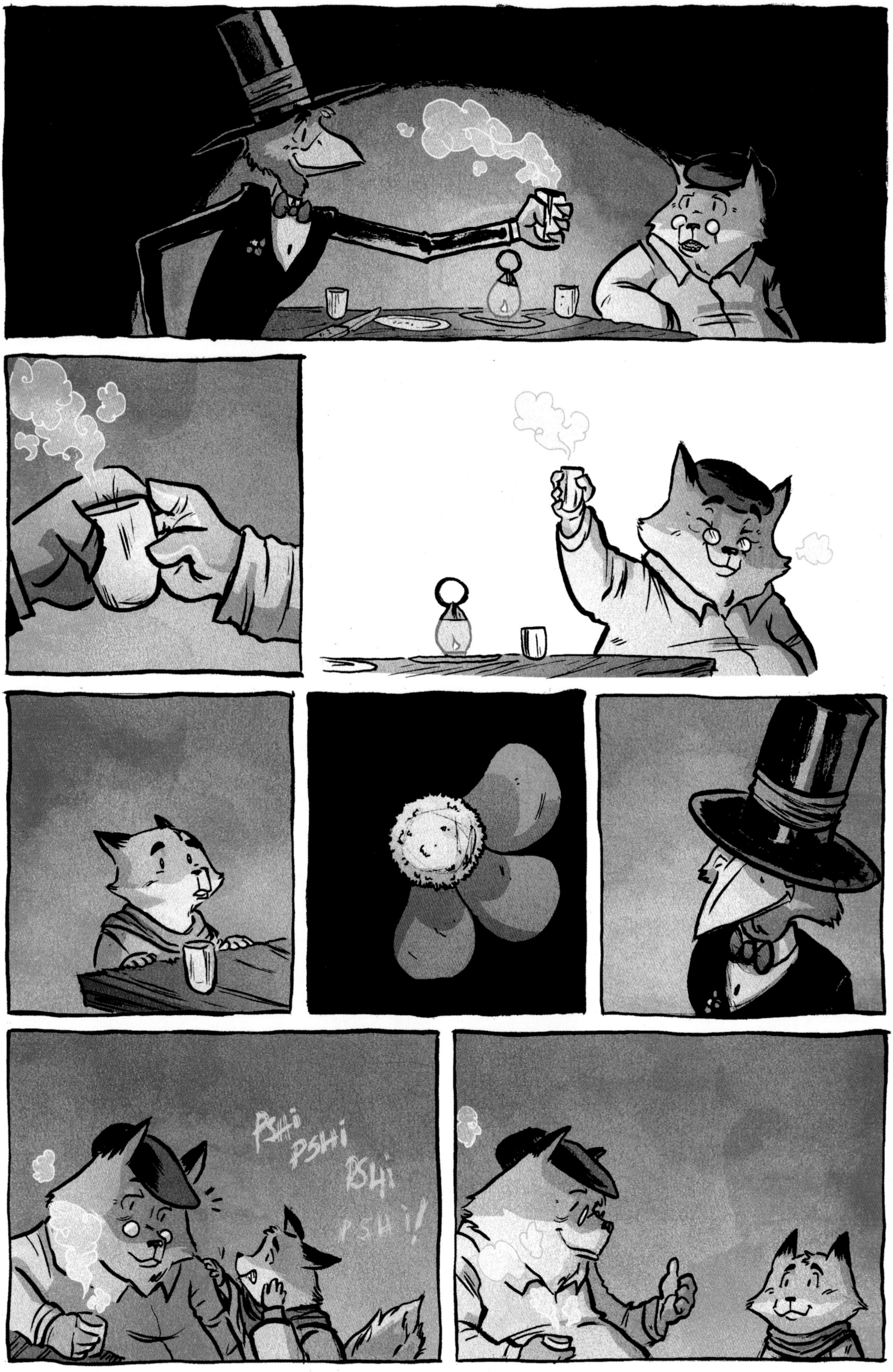
PSHI
PSHI
PSHI
PSHI!

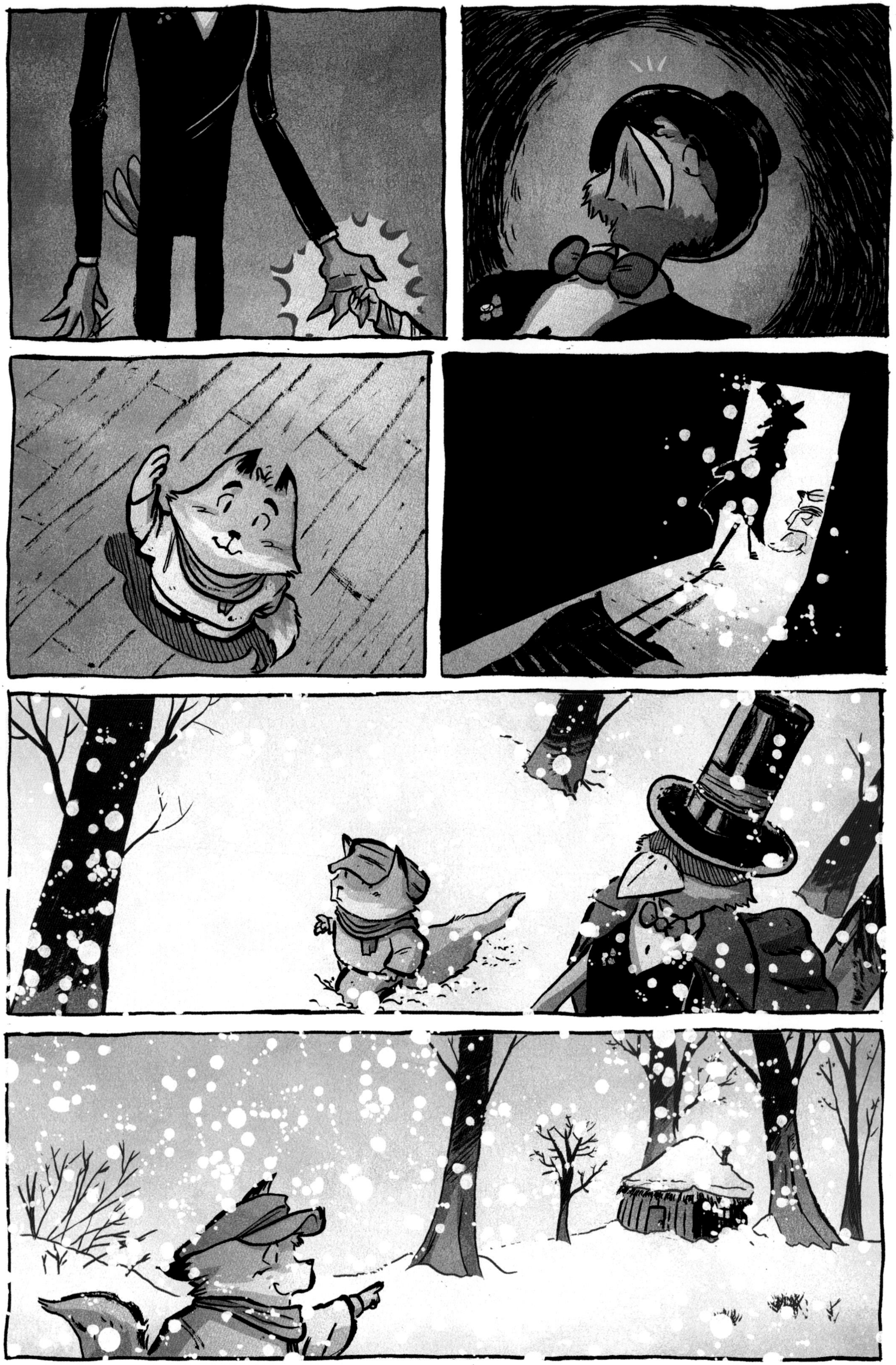

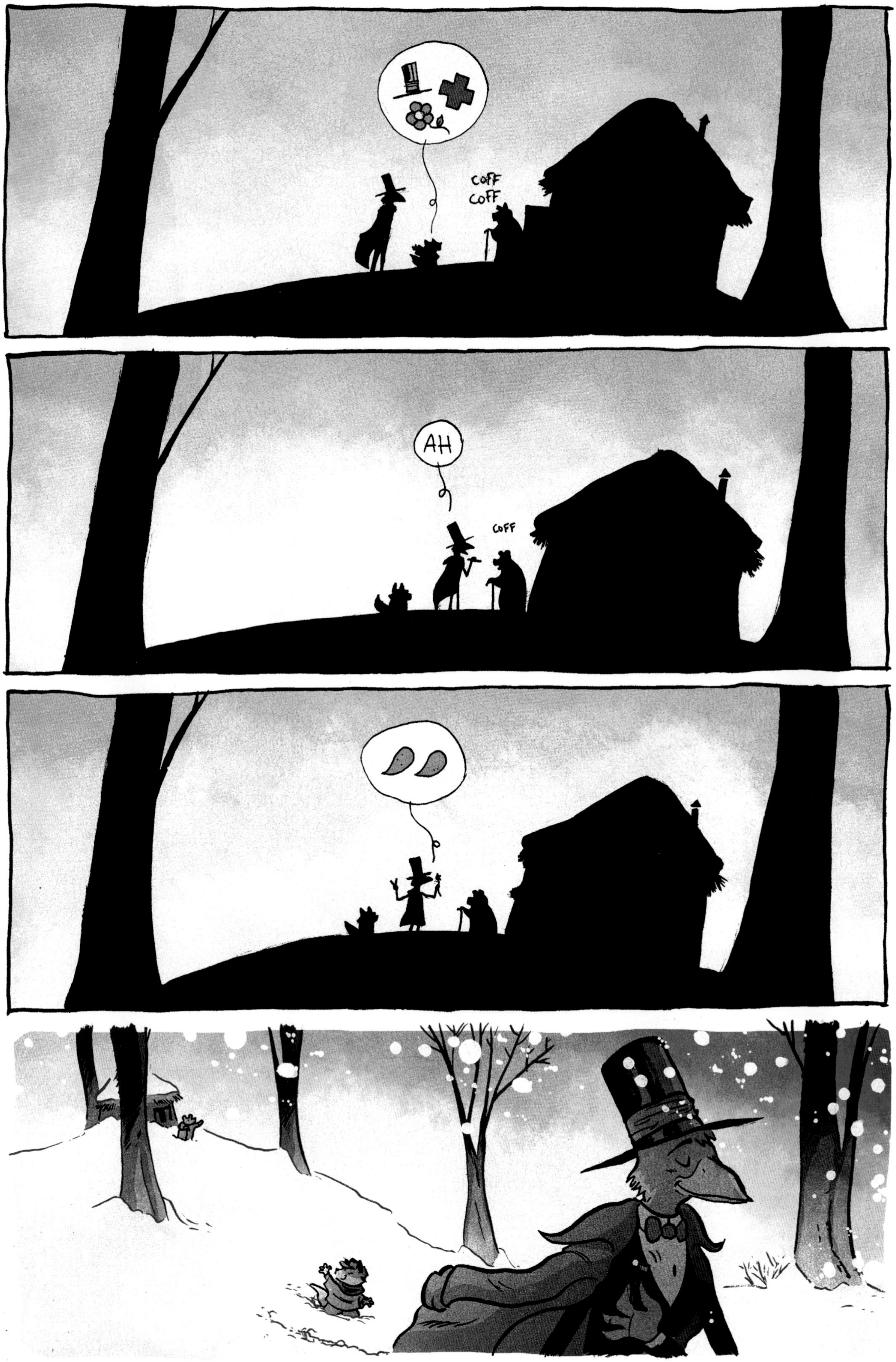
COFF
COFF
AH
COFF

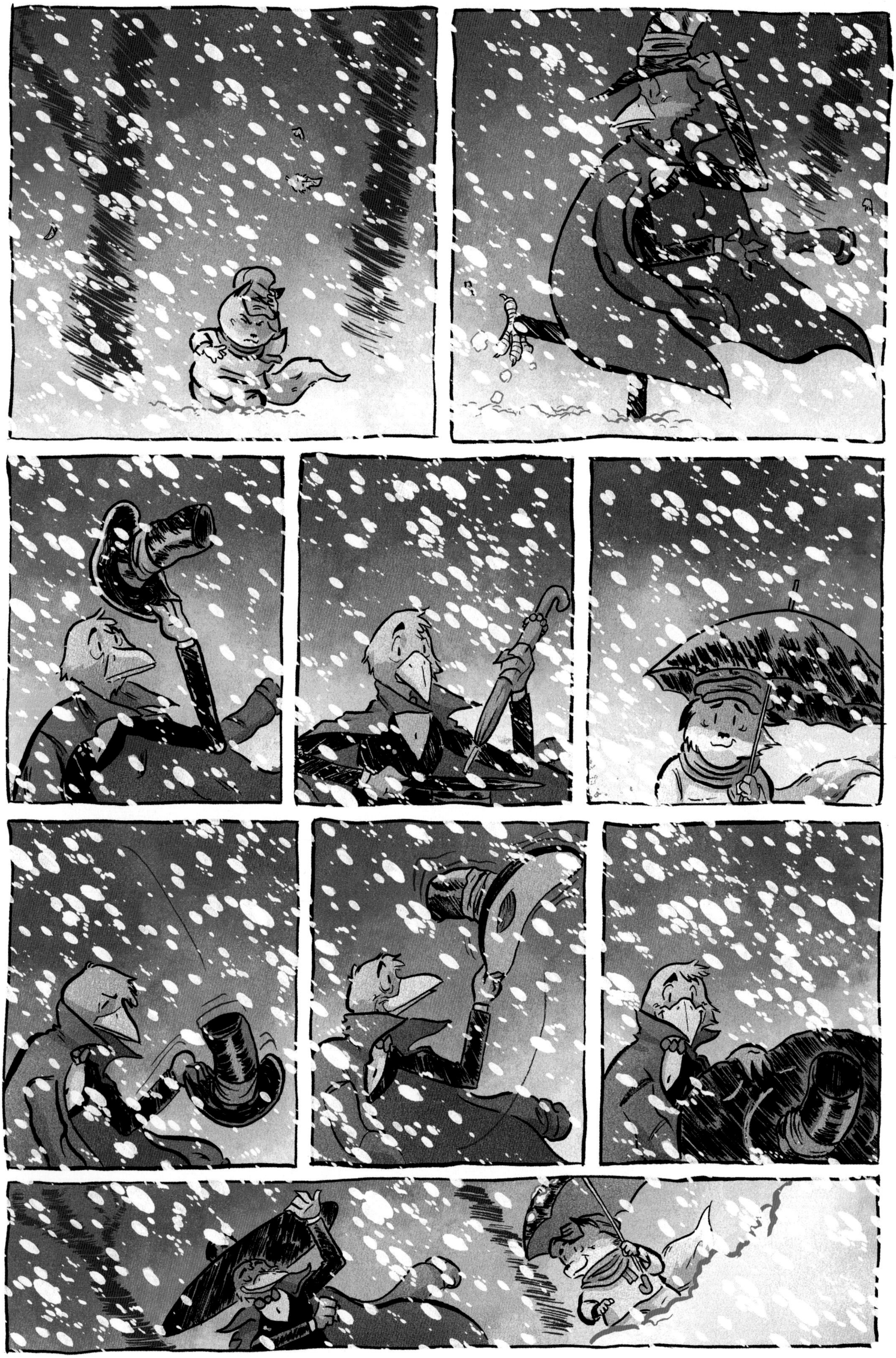

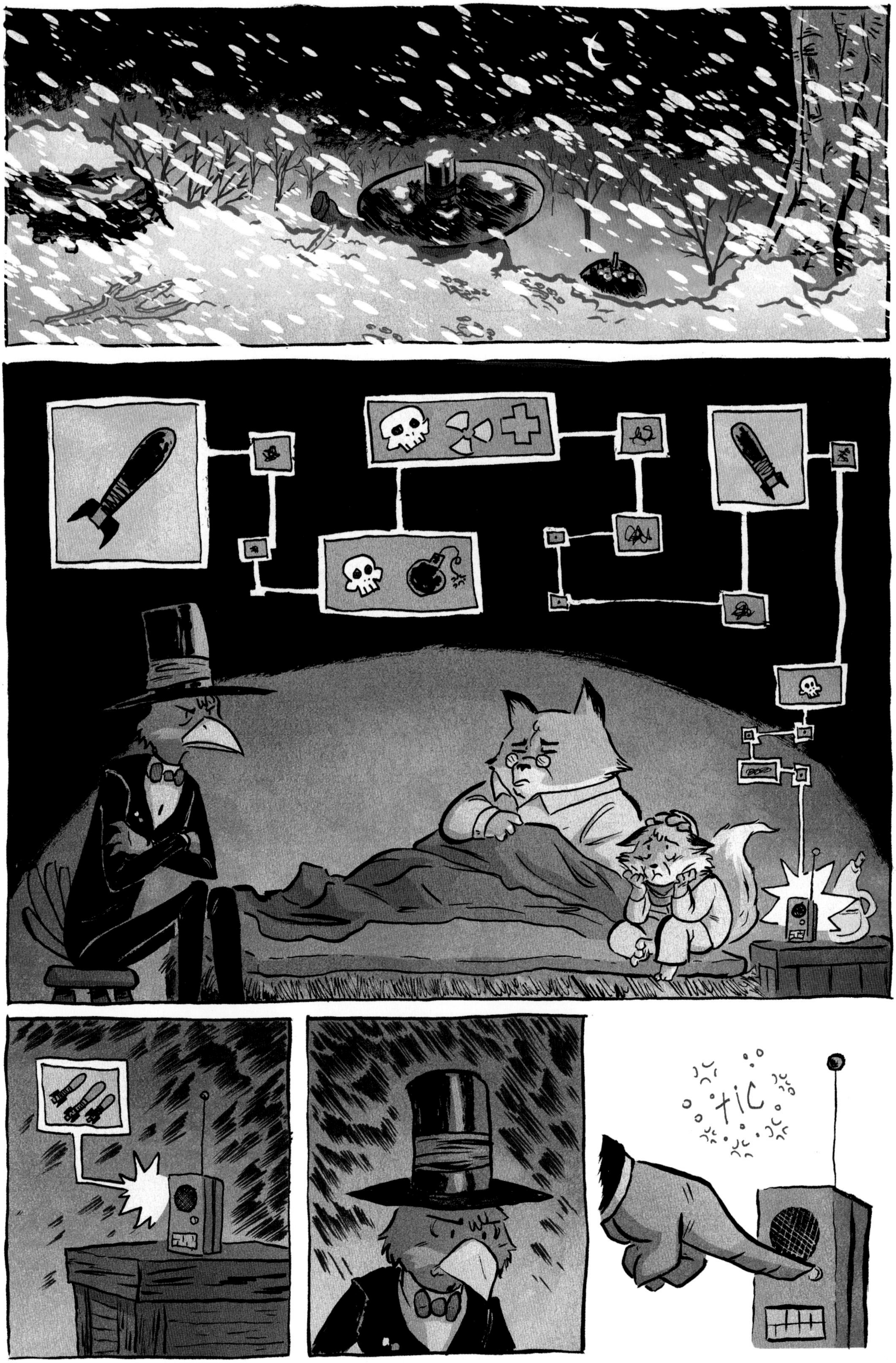
tic

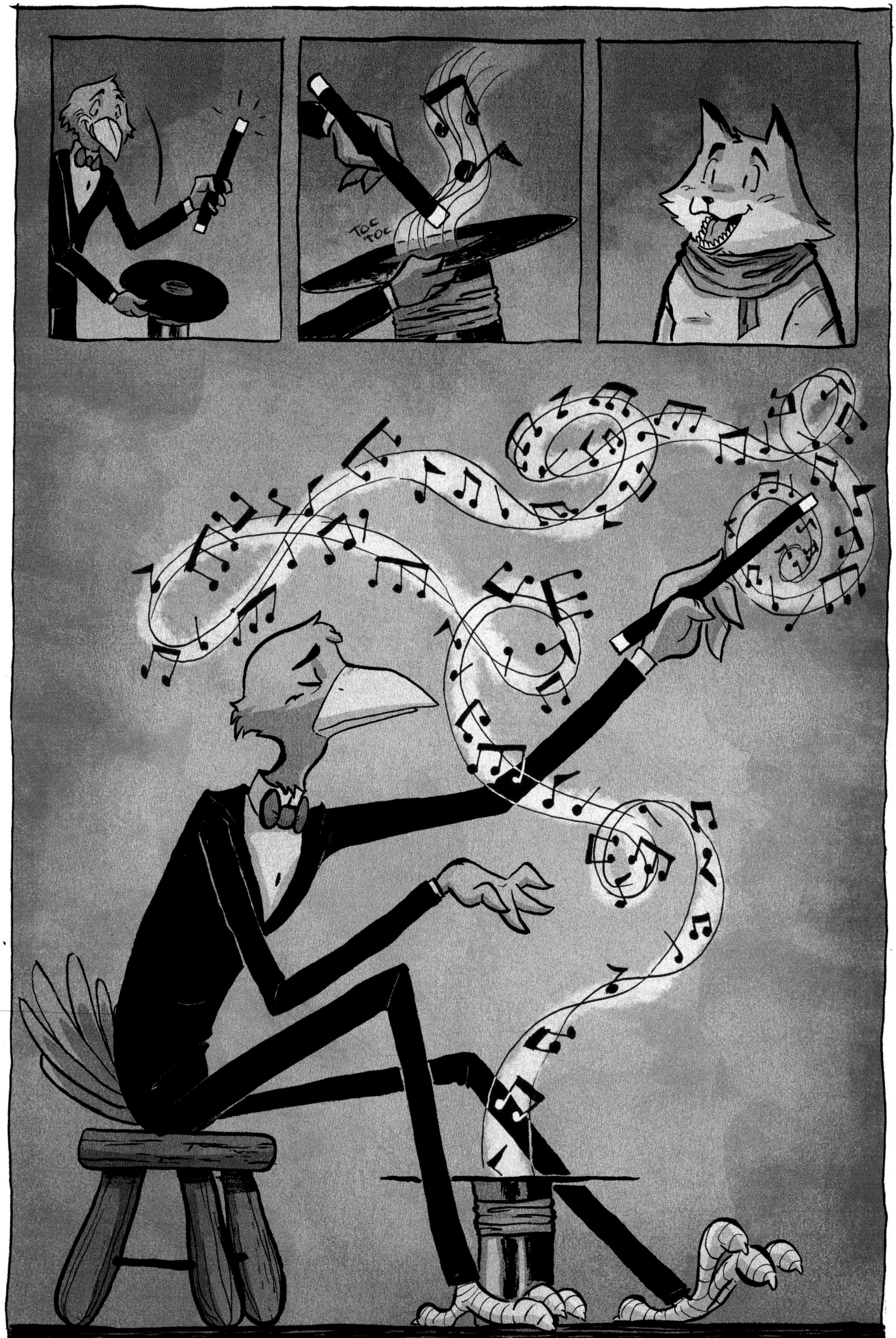
TOC
TOC

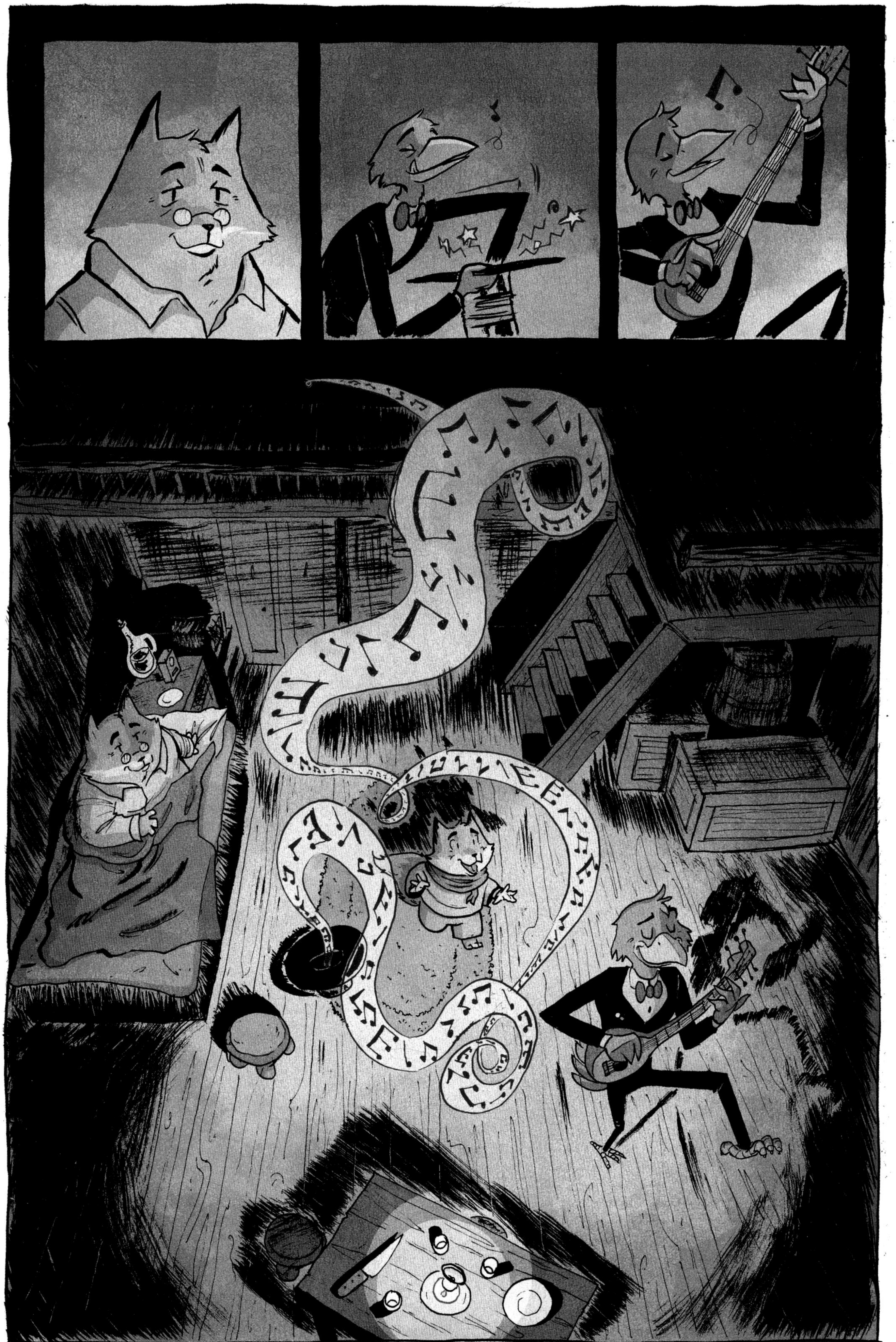

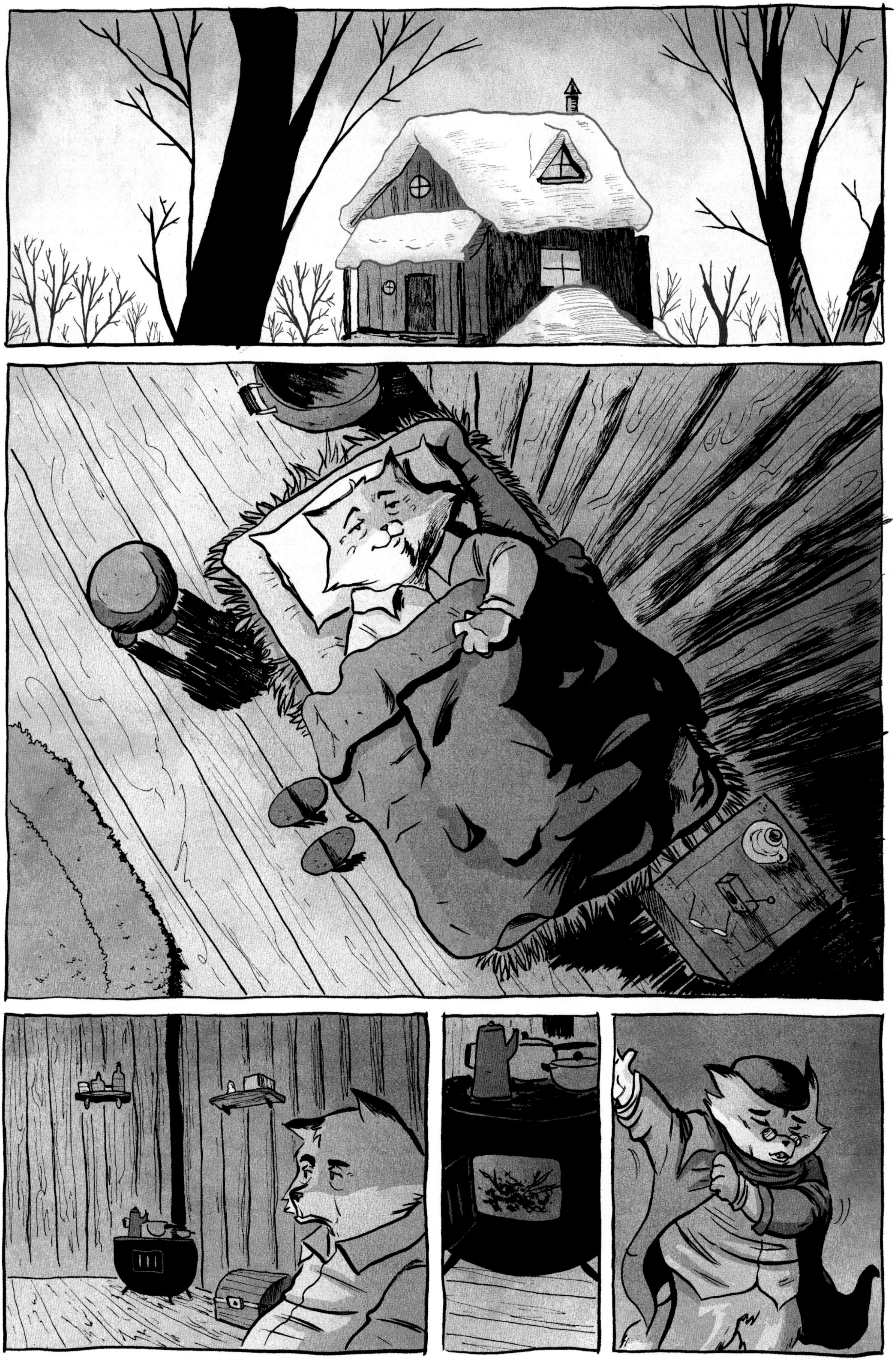

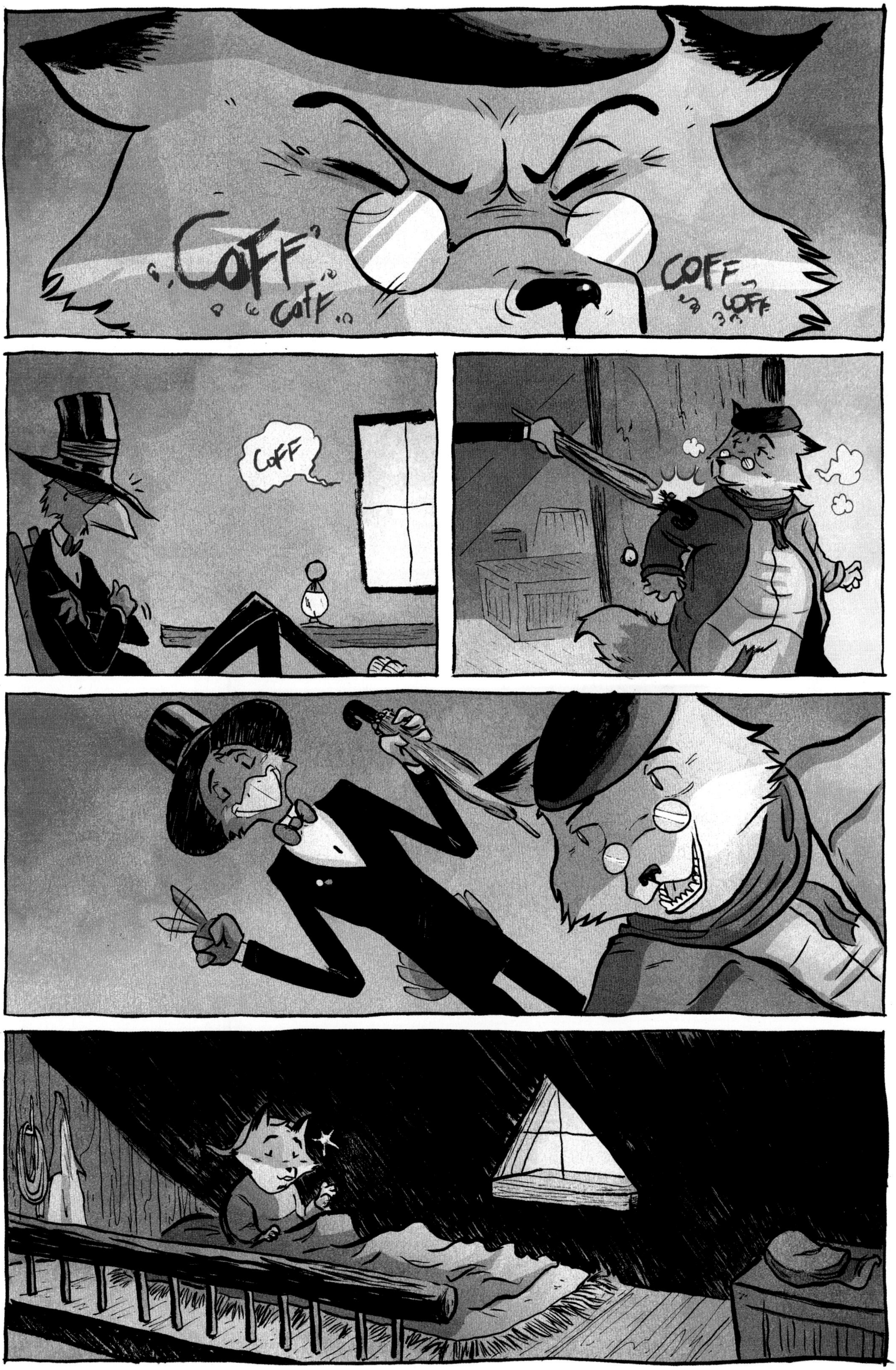
COFF
COFF
COFF
COFF
COFF

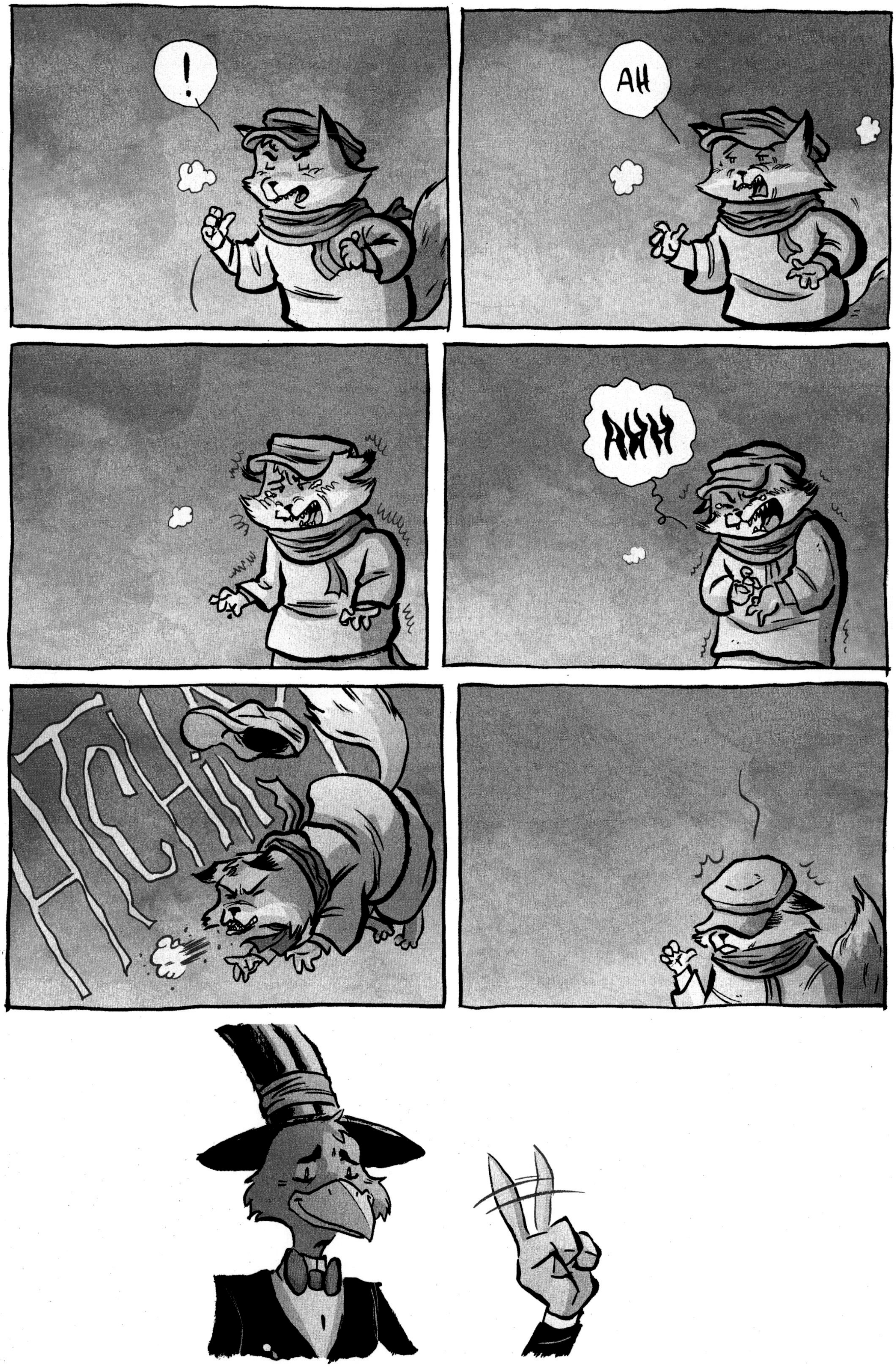
!
AH
AHH
ATCHI

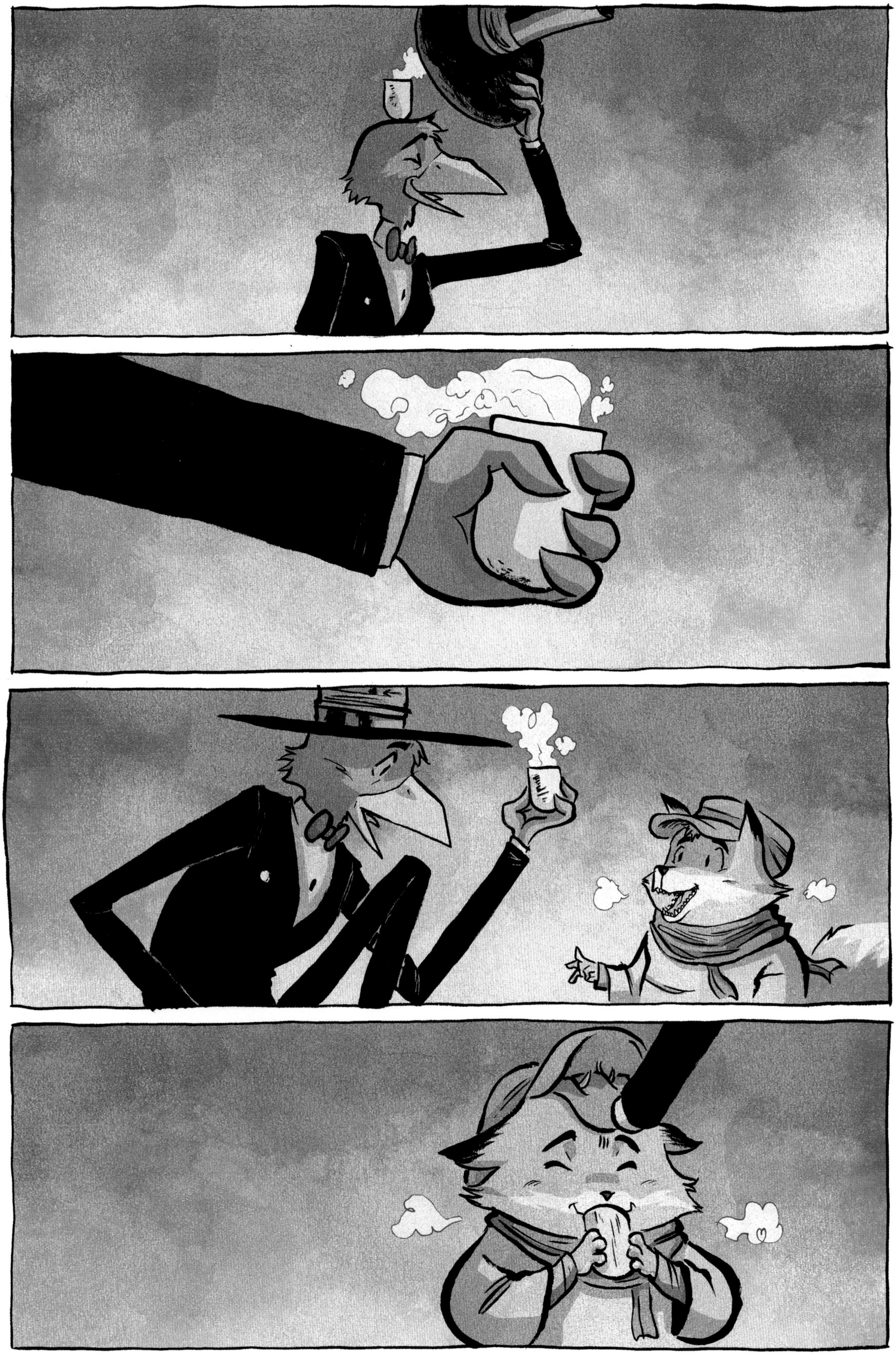

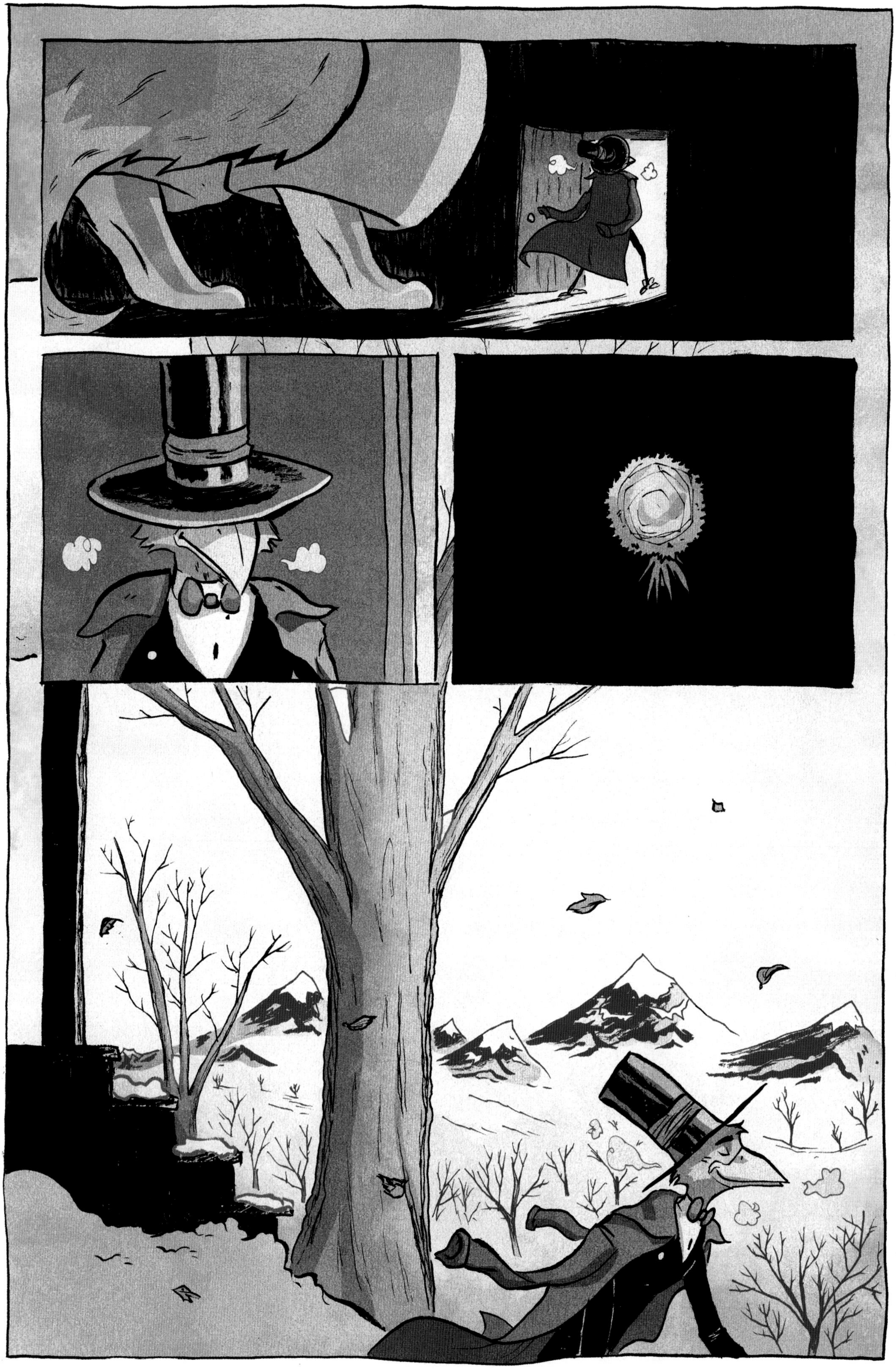

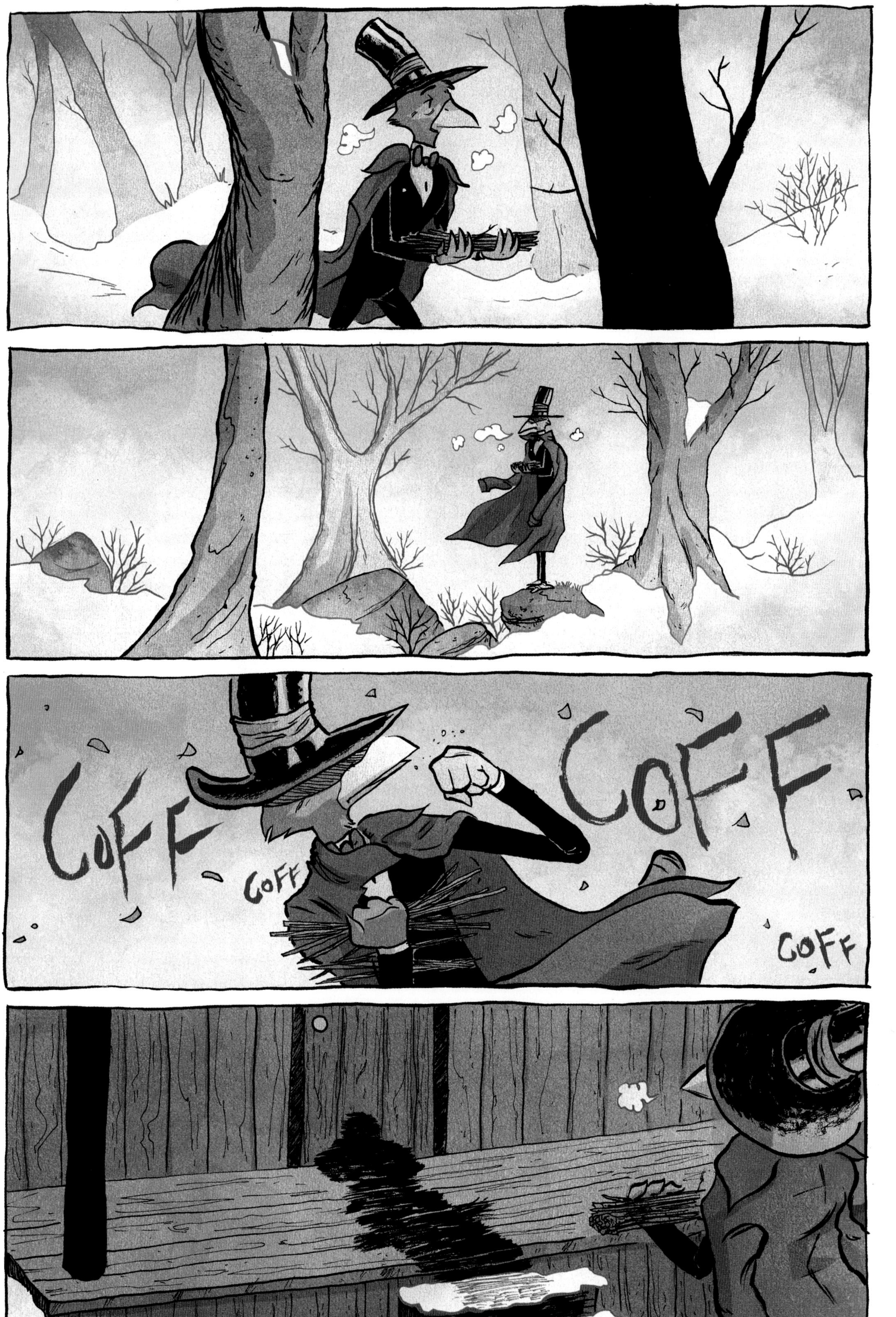
COFF
COFF
COFF
COFF

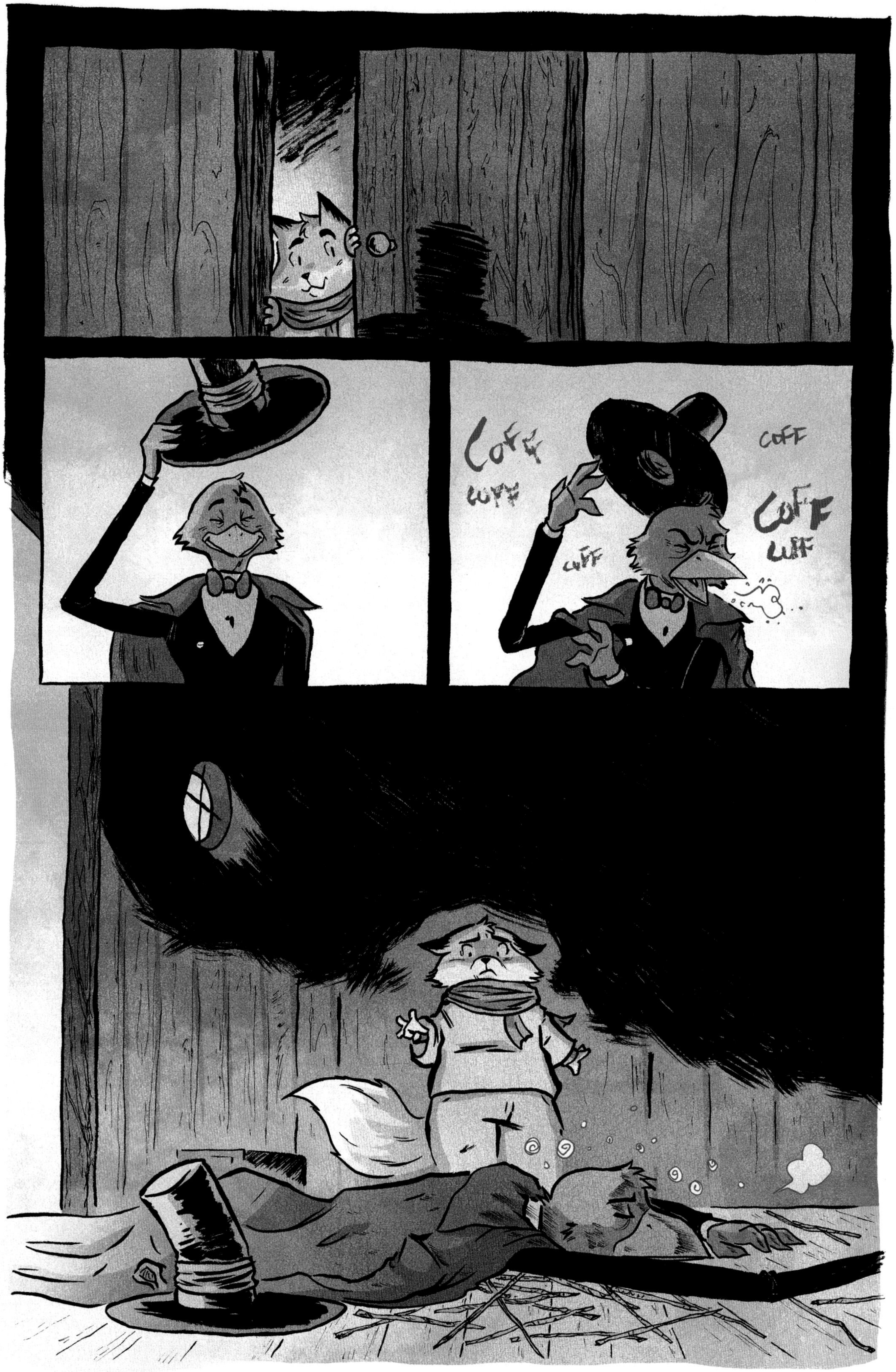
COFF
CUFF
CUFF
COFF
COFF
CUFF

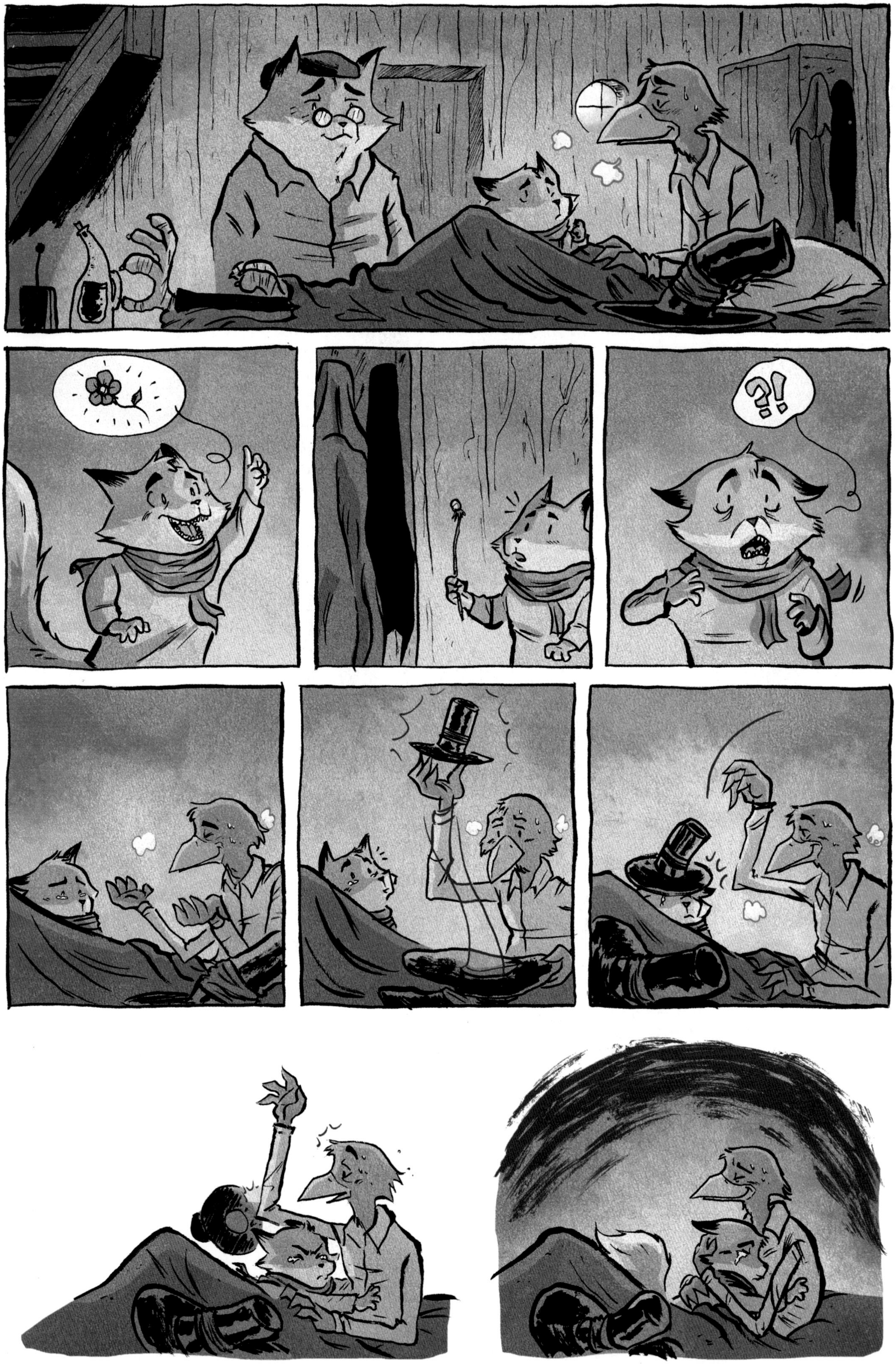
?!

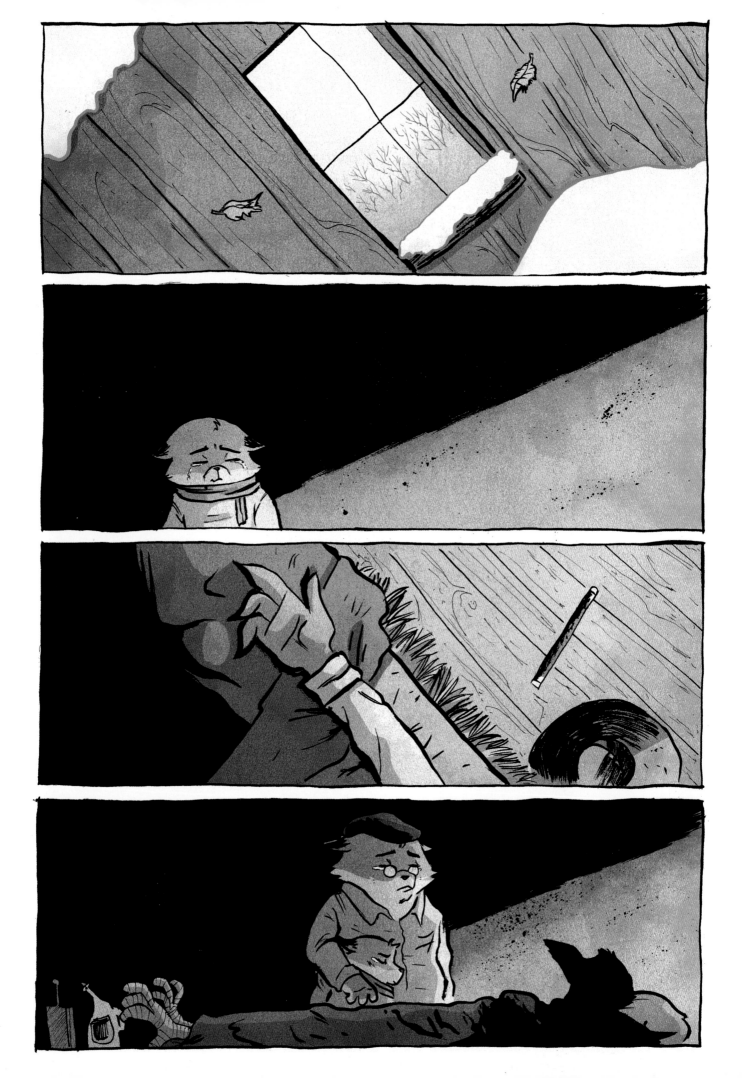

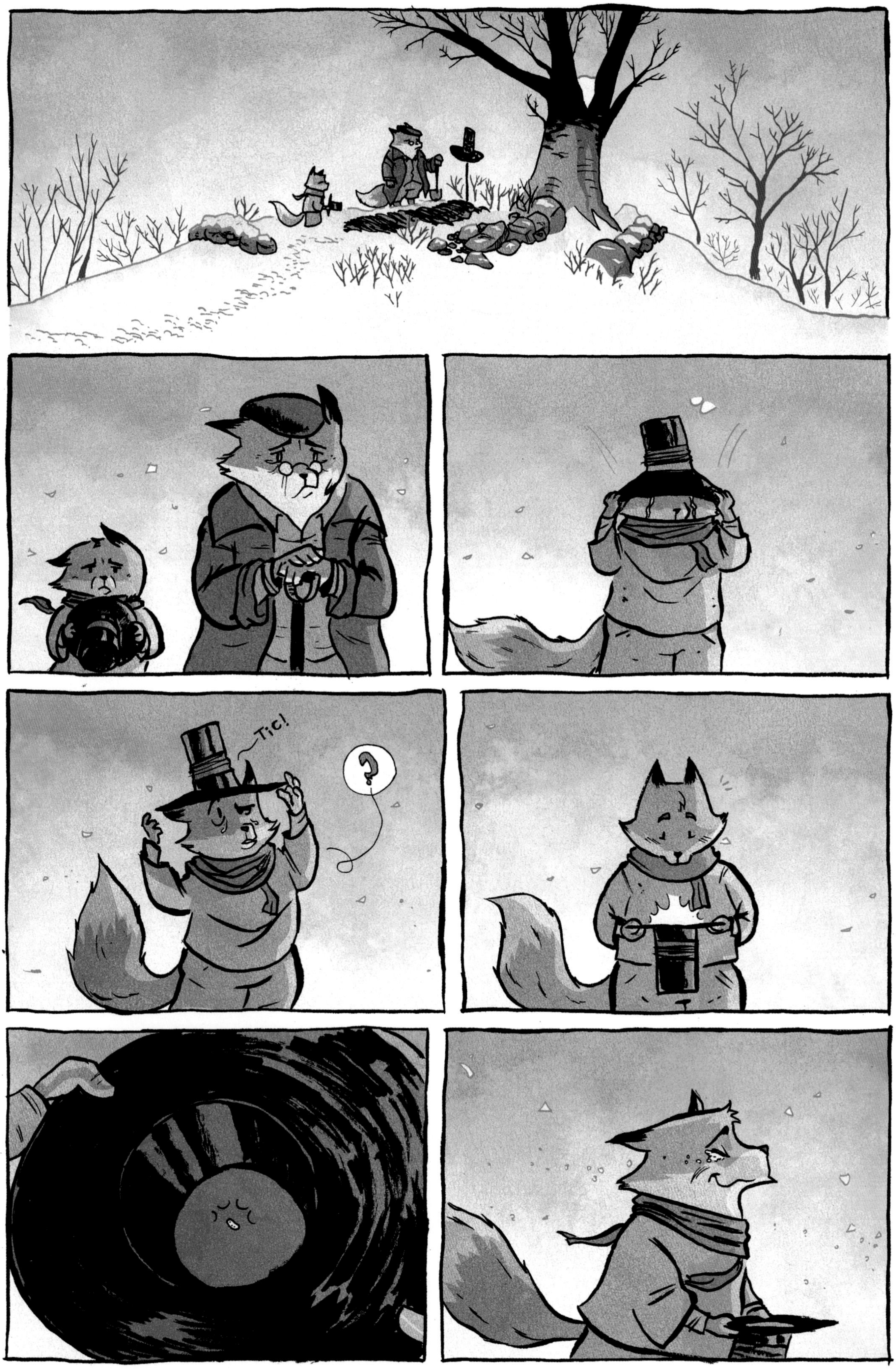
Tic!
?

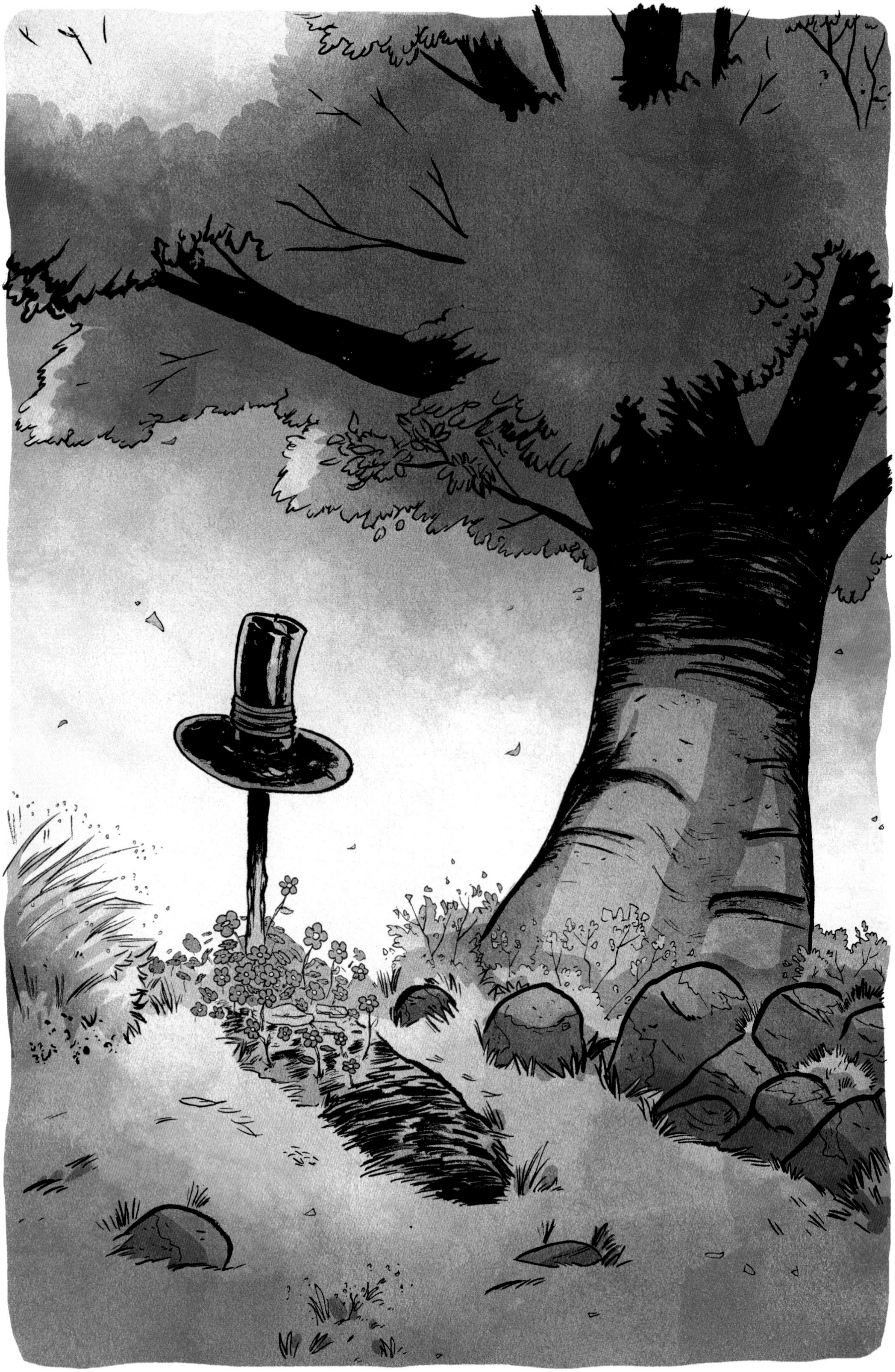

THE MAKING OF Petals™

WITH GUSTAVO BORGES

In the beginning, all I wanted was to draw a comic with a straightforward story in the traditional comic format. I had only ever done comic strips with my personal work and webcomics. I wanted to show the world that I could create a longer story and work in a different format than what they were used to seeing.

I started to sketch things that I wanted to draw and as the first image of *Petals* came to my mind, I instantly knew the story would be beautiful and stronger if I could tell it with no words. I was worried that without words, I would be limited when it came to character development but I decided to turn it into a challenge—which turned out great, because I learned a lot during the creative process—and soon I was writing the script, defining acts, and shaping the characters.

Petals was sketched on a small notebook that allowed me to read and test the pages with each turn. It was hard to work with the story at times because of the dialogue-free narrative. I didn't know, for instance, how to show the little Fox's reaction when he invites the Bird to his home, since he had to ask an adult before simply letting him into the house. You should always ask for permission first.

As I began to finalize individual panels, the solutions to my problems became simple. But before I got there, this scene was definitely one of the hardest to illustrate without dialogue. This page is the one that took me the most amount of time to bring to life but I was eventually able to figure out the actions and the flow of the page to get it to the place and pace that I wanted to give readers.

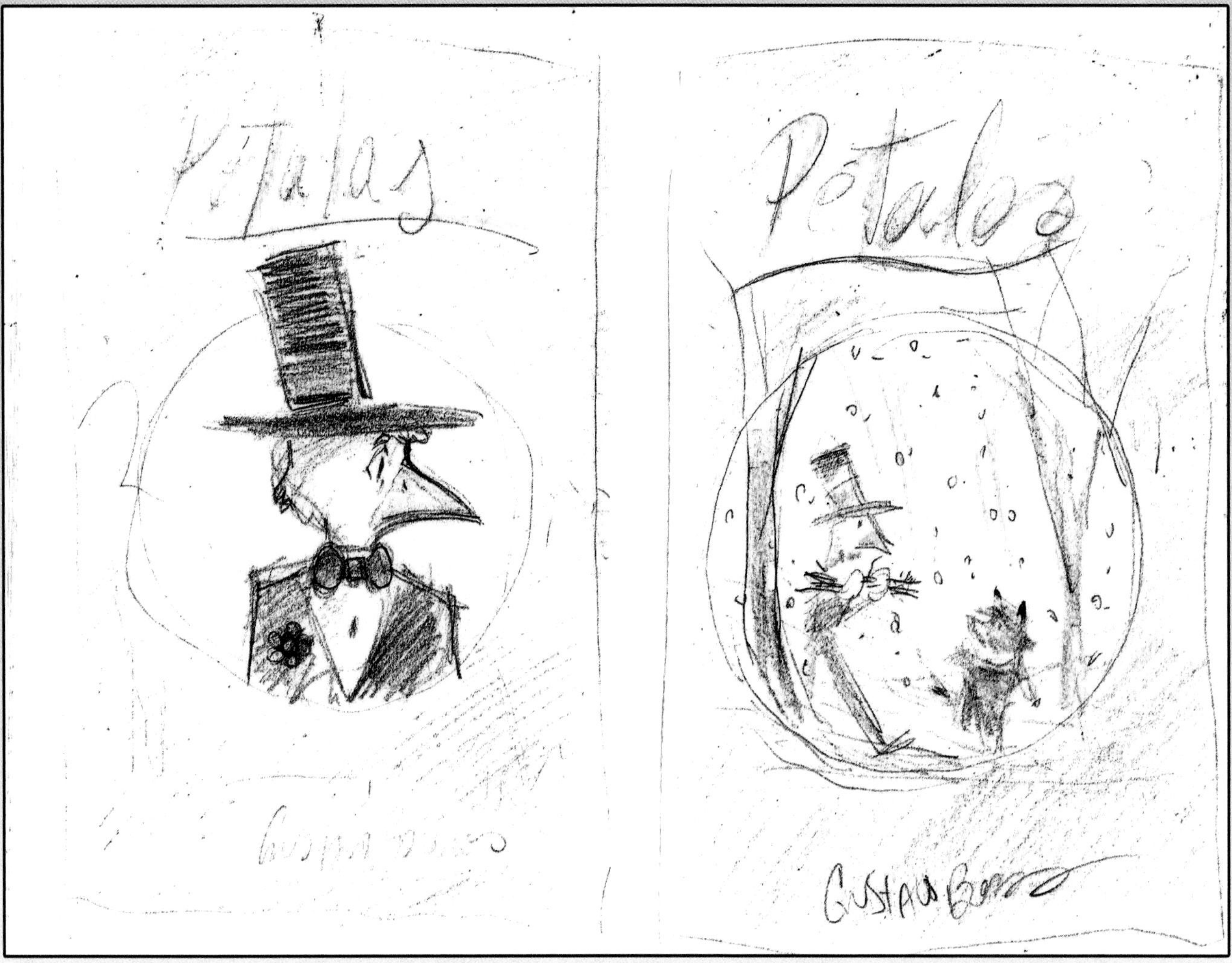
Pétalas
Pétalas

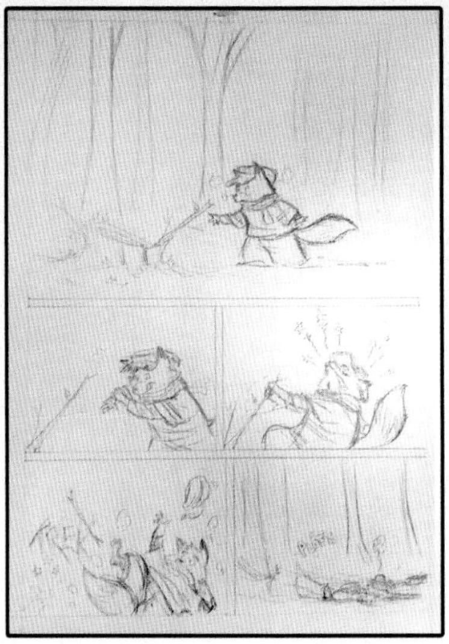

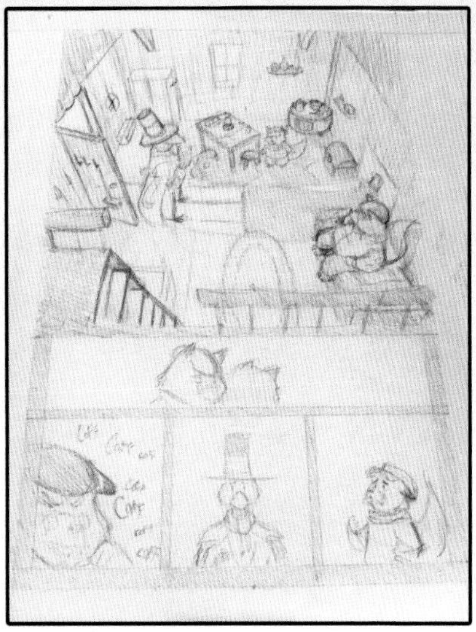

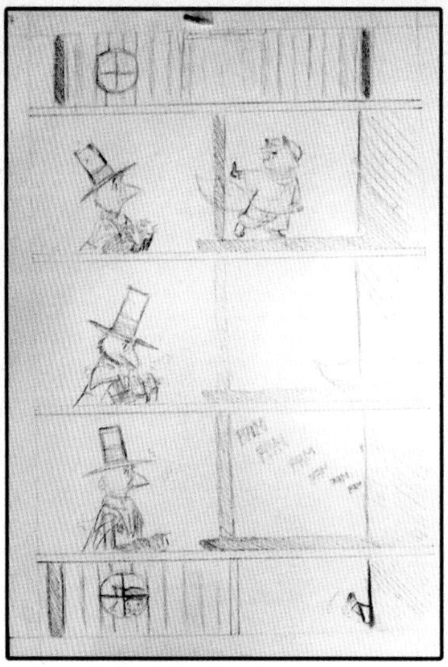

COLORING *Petals*™
WITH CRIS PETER

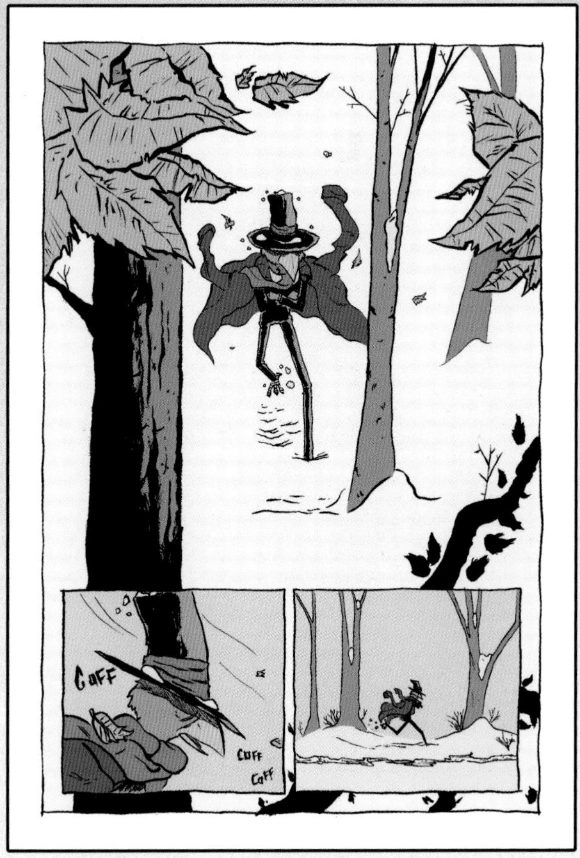
COFF
COFF
COFF

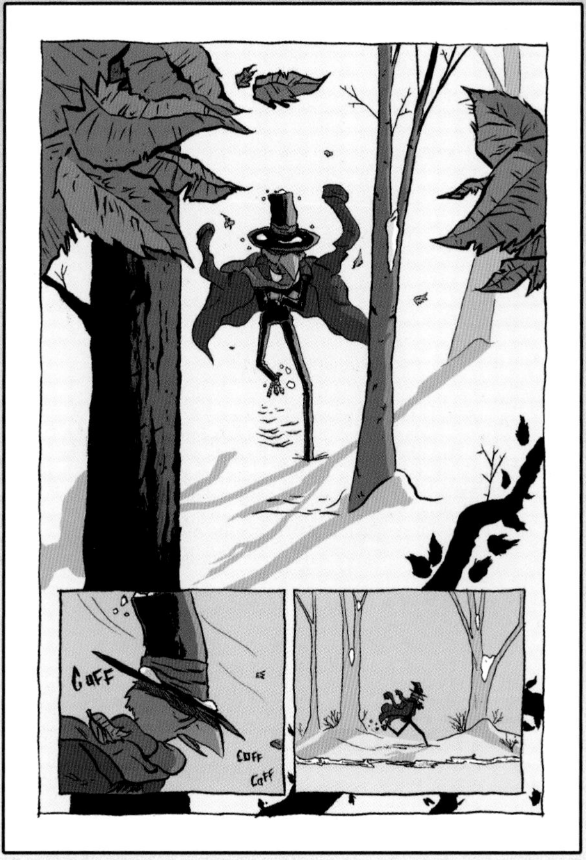
COFF
COFF
COFF

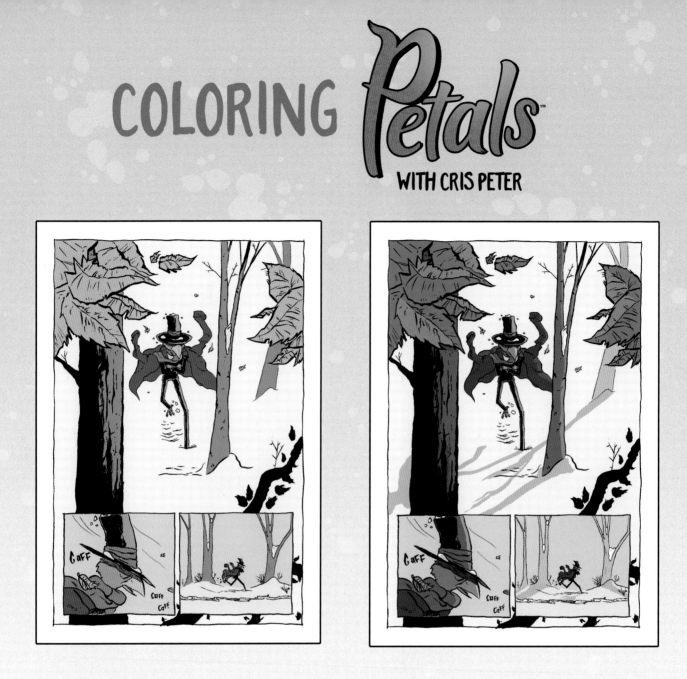

We were at Afonso Pena Airport in Curitiba waiting to our flight to Porto Alegre when Gustavo told me the story of *Petals*. It was right after we had shared a table at GibiCon 2014. I instantly started visualizing the colors for the pages that he had been able to show me, which were roughly sketched and photographed on his phone. I was excited to be involved with *Petals* because Gustavo's art is beautiful, the story is cute, and I had faith in the book that Gustavo wanted to put together.

When coloring, I try to define the base color palette of the page first. I like to use less saturated colors in the beginning and use more saturated colors over them in the process. Then, I apply the shades. I like to add cyan to darken the base colors and make hard shades without gradients. After that, I saturate the images a little. I apply the gradient tool in Photoshop and this leaves a new color effect which I love.

Eventually in the process, I played with the texture brushes on the snow and in the scenery. I was able to add a mist effect to help the air feel icy and then I continued to add texture to the page by creating some texture of my own. I scanned a sheet of paper previously brushed with India ink and added it digitally to help create the texture that you see now. Sorry that this is a little technical but I hope my explanation helps you understand my process a bit more.

GALLERY

ANA KOEHLER

EDUARDO DAMASCENO

VITOR & LU CABAGGI

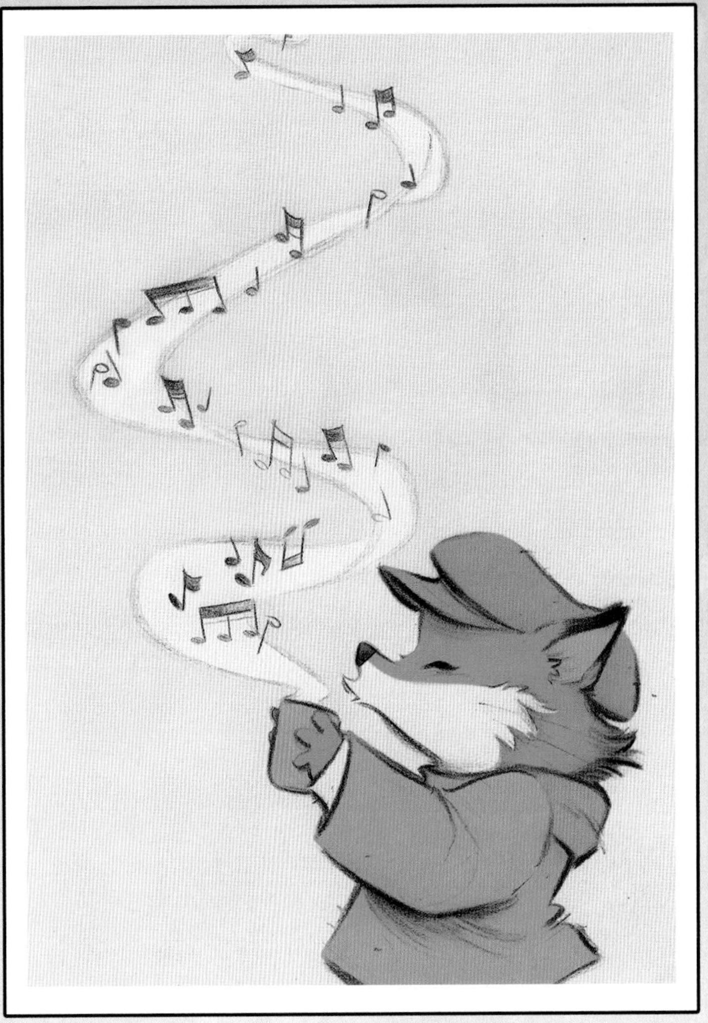

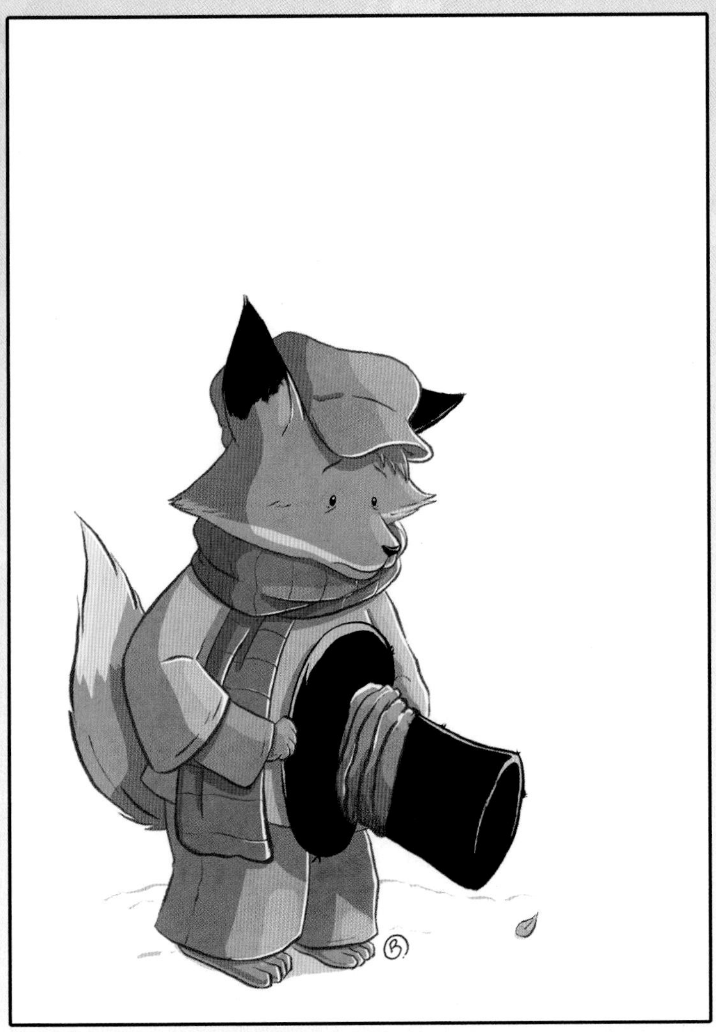

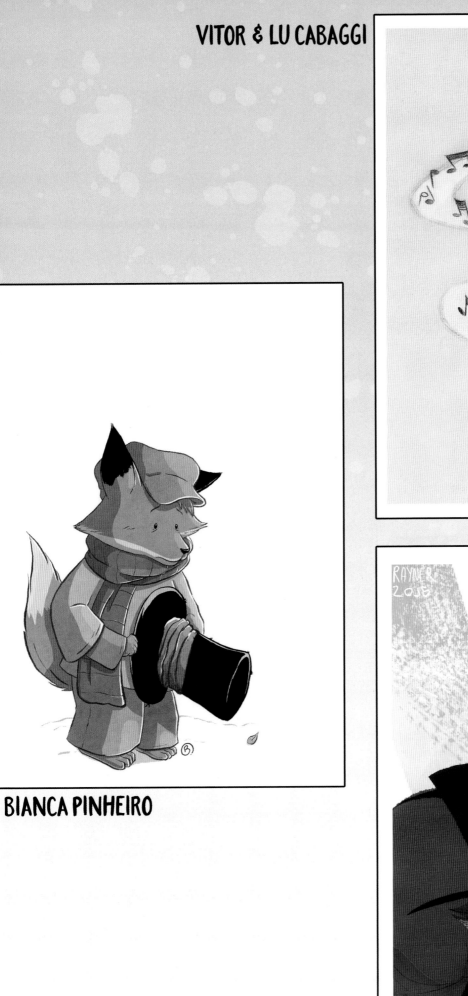

BIANCA PINHEIRO

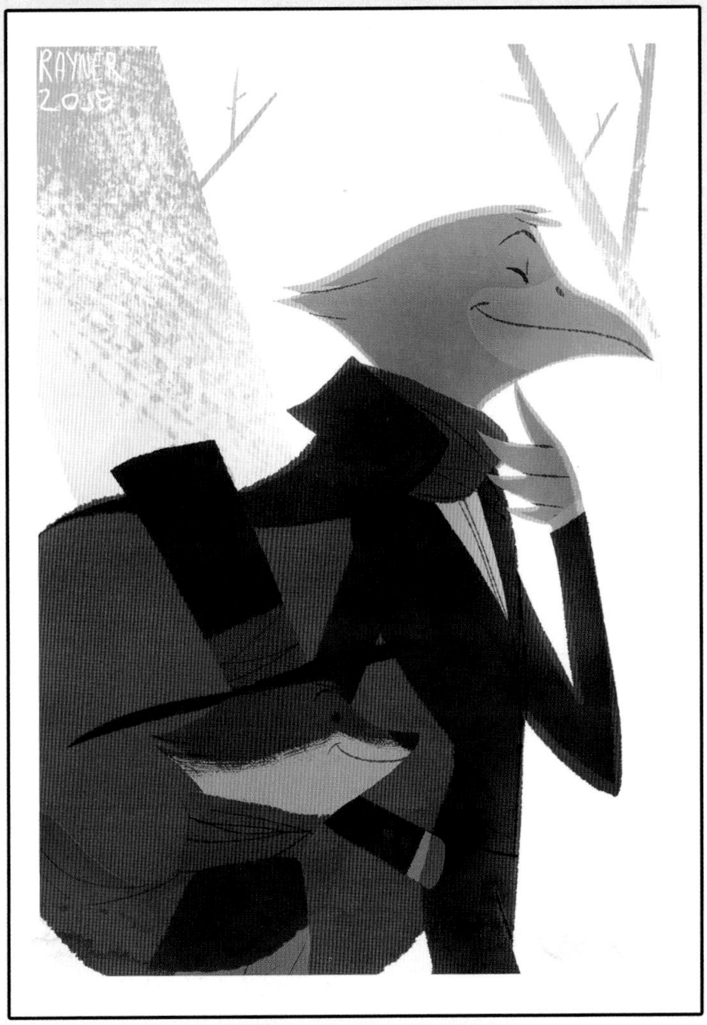

RAYNER ALENCAR

EDUARDO MEDEIROS

GUILHERME PETRECA

VENCYS LAO

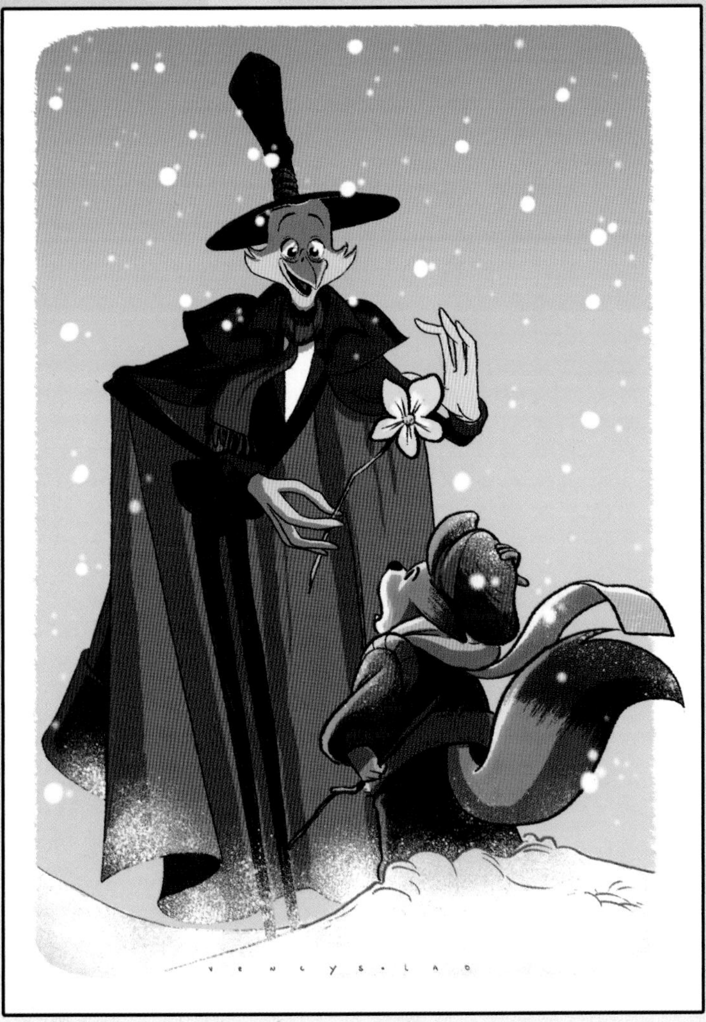
VENCYS LAO

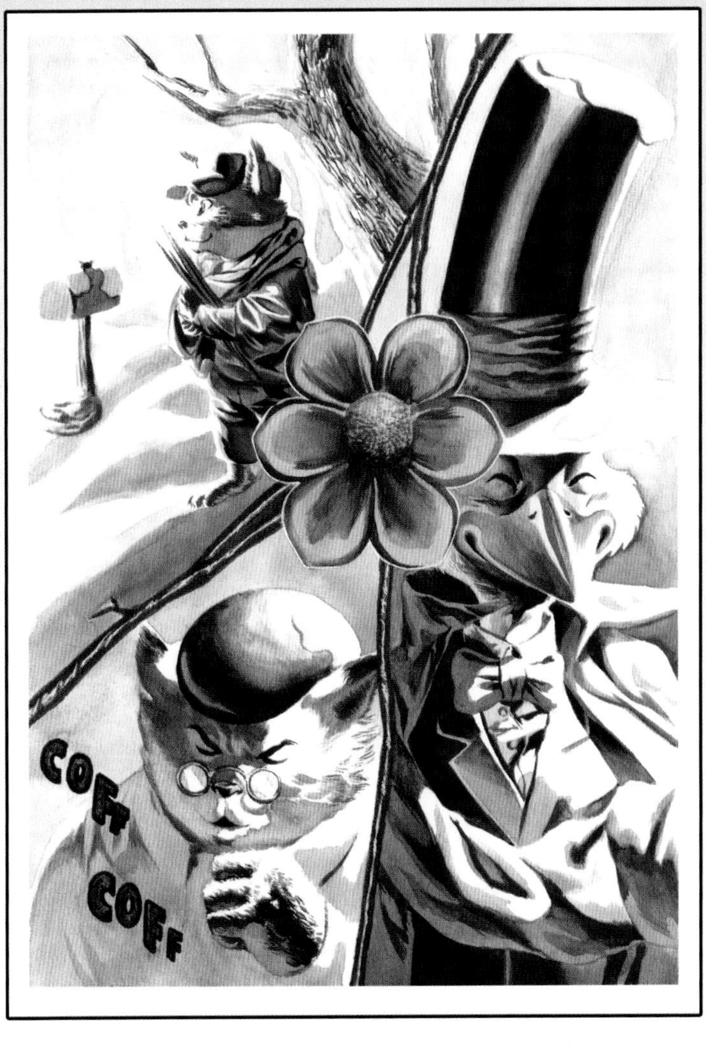
COFF
COFF

MATIAS STREB

GUSTAVO BORGES is a Brazilian cartoonist and creator of the webcomics *A Entediante Vida de Morte Crens* and *Edgar*. He has participated in publications such as *Memórias do Mauricio* and *321 Fast Comics*, in addition to publishing his own graphic novels such as *Escolhas* (with Felipe Cagno, published by Geektopia), and *Até o Fim* (with Eric Peleias and Michel Ramalho, published by Geektopia). In 2015, Gustavo won the Troféu HQ Mix in the category of "Best Independent Publication" for his first *Edgar* strip collection. Gustavo is currently working on his next graphic novel and is excited to continue to share his stories with the world.

CRIS PETER was born in 1983, Porto Alegre, Brazil, where she still lives and works from home. She majored in Advertising and with a postgraduate degree in Communication and Strategic Marketing As a colorist, she worked for titles such as *Superman/Batman, Batgirl, We Are Robin* with DC Comics and has worked on *Astonishing X-Men* and *Fantastic Four* with Marvel Comics. Cris was nominated for the Eisner Awards in 2012 for her work on *Casanova*, written by Matt Fraction and illustrated by Gabriel Bá and Fábio Moon.

DISCOVER
EXPLOSIVE NEW WORLDS

ADVENTURE TIME

sam sykes · selina espiritu · sarah stern
BRAVE CHEF BRIANNA

KELLY THOMPSON BRIANNE DROUHARD M. VICTORIA ROBADO
MEGA PRINCESS

THE NOT-SO SECRET SOCIETY
DALEY · CRAFTS · CLARK · BRUNI
KEEP OUT
CAUTION

OVER THE GARDEN WALL

STEVEN UNIVERSE
VOLUME ONE

kaboom!™

AVAILABLE AT YOUR LOCAL COMICS SHOP AND BOOKSTORE

To find a comics shop in your area, call 1-888-266-4226

WWW.**BOOM-STUDIOS**.COM

Adventure Time
Pendleton Ward and Others
Volume 1
ISBN: 978-1-60886-280-1 | $14.99 US
Volume 2
ISBN: 978-1-60886-323-5 | $14.99 US
Adventure Time: Islands
ISBN: 978-1-60886-972-5 | $9.99 US

The Amazing World of Gumball
Ben Bocquelet and Others
Volume 1
ISBN: 978-1-60886-488-1 | $14.99 US
Volume 2
ISBN: 978-1-60886-793-6 | $14.99 US

Brave Chef Brianna
Sam Sykes, Selina Espiritu
ISBN: 978-1-68415-050-2 | $14.99 US

Mega Princess
Kelly Thompson, Brianne Drouhard
ISBN: 978-1-68415-007-6 | $14.99 US

The Not-So Secret Society
Matthew Daley, Arlene Daley, Wook Jin Clark
ISBN: 978-1-60886-997-8 | $9.99 US

Over the Garden Wall
Patrick McHale, Jim Campbell and Others
Volume 1
ISBN: 978-1-60886-940-4 | $14.99 US
Volume 2
ISBN: 978-1-68415-006-9 | $14.99 US

Steven Universe
Rebecca Sugar and Others
Volume 1
ISBN: 978-1-60886-706-6 | $14.99 US
Volume 2
ISBN: 978-1-60886-796-7 | $14.99 US

Steven Universe & The Crystal Gems
ISBN: 978-1-60886-921-3 | $14.99 US

Steven Universe: Too Cool for School
ISBN: 978-1-60886-771-4 | $14.99 US

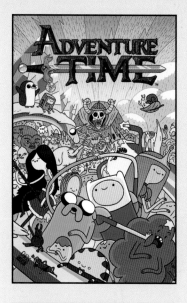

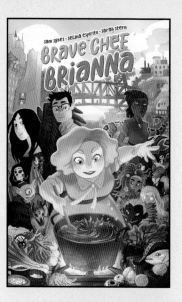

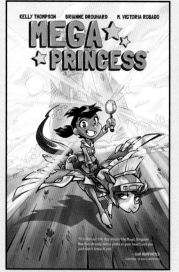

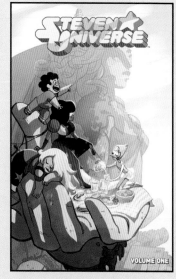

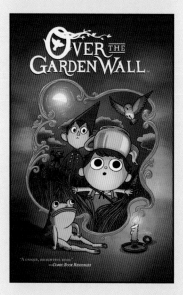

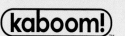

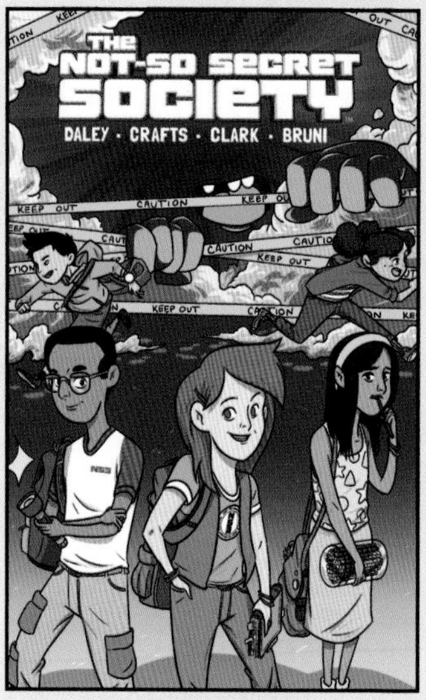